LOST AND ALONE

A Novel

Bill Jack

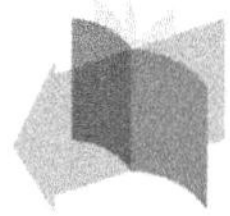

Chapbook Press

Schuler Books
2660 28th Street SE
Grand Rapids, MI 49512
(616) 942-7330
www.schulerbooks.com

ISBN 13: 9781948327260

Library of Congress Control Number: 2019905332

Cover Art by Rebecca Sitterly

Printed in the United States by Chapbook Press.

Dedication

To my beautiful sister, Mary Sue Jack, who played the ultimate dirtiest trick on her little brother by dying before I did. That is not the way I planned it.

To me, she was my goofy older sister but to so many others, she was much greater than that. A hospital nurse, then a nursing professor, then Assistant Dean of Student Affairs at the University of Rochester and always a committed woman of the world and of reproductive rights for all humans. And committed especially to the men and women of the Memorial Art Gallery in Rochester who she loved with all her heart.

Every phone call from her would start with: "Oh hi, Bill, it's me. Your sister."

And so, my dearest friend, to you: "Oh hi, Mary Sue, it's your little brother. Thank you for everything you accomplished in this world of ours and thank you for being the best sister ever. I miss you."

Acknowledgments

To my bride, Rebecca Sitterly, a quester, whose career has taken her from lawyer to judge to nurse to paramedic and back to lawyer. Above all she is an artist who has never seen a medium she can't conquer. I am in awe of her talent and her energy but, most of all, in awe of the fact she still loves me.

To daughter, Kate, whose courage and generosity and kindness of spirit have led her on a journey to save the world, one person at a time. I have no doubt she will succeed and, in doing so, is an inspiration to all whose lives she touches like no other that I have ever encountered.

Chapter One

Aftermath

She stopped her police car at the top of the driveway and surveyed the scene. Three Black and Whites cluttered the driveway with lights flashing and uniformed patrol officers in various degrees of "at rest" positions. Yellow police tape surrounded the dilapidated, adobe structure that was officially now a homicide crime scene. The house itself was in major need of a lot of deferred maintenance and did not look loved by any stretch of her imagination. The yard surrounding the house was a mess, littered with trash, beer cans, and whiskey bottles. A rusted out Ford pickup was on blocks just to the left of the main house. And those were just the things she could identify. She saw three outbuildings behind the main structure that was taped off.

Margaret Espinoza, Chief of Homicide for the Albuquerque Police Department, had been called to the scene by the responding officers who had been dispatched after an anonymous 911 call that claimed a disturbance at the house located in a remote part of the South Valley of Albuquerque. The South Valley was no stranger to the Albuquerque Police Department. While there were a number of hard working families in the north of the Valley and farming at the far south, the area south of Kirtland Air Force Base was riddled with drug and gang violence and had been for years.

And it was in the South Valley that her son, Ronnie, had been killed some months before. She felt a shiver, then drove the rest of the way down the driveway.

Upon arrival, the first two responding officers had found three men in the living room in various states of drug incoherence, drug paraphernalia on the tables, amid pizza remains and fast food boxes. Two of the three who were still conscious had professed their innocence to the officers of anything other than hanging with the guys and agreed the officers could search the rest of the house "because we got nothing to hide."

Which was a bit of a stretch. In one of three bedrooms, the officers found a very dead fourth man, lying on his back on the bed, with a very large bullet hole between his eyes, and a crude capital "M" carved into his chest. His shirt had been ripped open to gain access to the flesh and his jeans had been pulled down to his knees. The decedent apparently had decided to go Rambo on his last day on Earth. The two patrol officers called for backup and went back to the living room, stood guard over the three men and waited for help. As soon as reinforcements arrived, the three were separated and put in the back seats of separate squad cars. They had roused the third man just long enough to get him in the car where he promptly fell over and went back to sleep.

Margaret Espinoza was a veteran of the Albuquerque Police Department and had worked her way up from being one of the first woman patrol officers to Chief of Homicide. She had done it through guts and determination, endured the sexism rampant in the Department when she had started, endured recriminations from her fellow officers on failed investigations, endured the death of her only son, and persevered. Six months before, she was promoted to her current post and there was talk that, at some point, she would be a candidate for Chief of Police. She got out of the police car on this beautiful New Mexico not a cloud in the sky early September afternoon and put her game face on.

As she got closer, she was met by Sergeant Jorge Rodriguez who was in charge of the scene until her arrival. Margaret had known him for years and they had that easy familiarity that comes from mutual respect and admiration and having had each other's back on many many occasions. She was pleased he was in charge as all would be done by the book. No mistakes would be made on his watch.

"What do we have, Jorge?" Never one to stand on the formality of rank.

"One dead in the bedroom with a huge hole in his forehead from at least a .45 caliber, a huge "M" carved in his chest, three druggies in the living room who know nothing about how the guy got dead, never heard a gunshot, and claimed to have been watching television all afternoon getting high."

"ID on the dead guy?"

Rodriguez pulled his spiral note pad from his shirt pocket. "Pablo Jiménez, brother of José Jiménez, one of the surviving stoners."

"Know anything else about him?"

"Nope and more questions than answers. No sign of a gun, no sign of a struggle, only thing the witnesses claim to know is Pablo got up to go to the bathroom and never came back."

"How long gone?"

"None of them have any idea."

By now more Black and Whites had arrived on the scene and Espinoza told Rodriguez to get the three druggies down to headquarters and keep them separated in interview rooms until she got back. Within minutes, the Medical Examiner rolled up in her black station wagon and got out with two of her assistants. Betty Warner had been the ME for Bernalillo County forever. No nonsense to the core and all about the business at hand. Espinoza and Rodriguez filled her in and led her into the house. Espinoza immediately started breathing through her mouth given the stench of the house. It wasn't the smell of death that made her sick because she had been around the smell of death too much in her career. It was the overwhelming odor of decay. Like animals had died and their rotting corpses lay where they'd died; like food had been left out on the counter tops for weeks on end until the mold had consumed whatever it had been weeks before; all mingled with the body odor of men who had not washed in weeks, if not months. No question in her mind or anybody else's that day that they had happened on a very bad drug house that hadn't seen a vacuum or a dust mop in years. She was certain that a full search would find something akin to a manufacturing facility. She had been to too many crime scenes that looked and smelled like this one. Only this was even worse.

In the back bedroom, the corpse was as the responding officers had found him and Warner went to work. The Detective and Sergeant left her and her team to do what they needed to do. Other detectives arrived and began a search of the premises.

In twenty minutes, Warner came out of the bedroom with a paper face mask on, took it off, and reported on the preliminary findings.

"Well, he's dead, pretty sure of that." Margaret put it off to ME humor.

"And?"

"Autopsy will confirm it for sure but cause of death is the gunshot to the head and no exit wound. Time of death probably within last two to three hours given the state of the rigor mortis. "M" on his chest likely done after he was shot, given depth of the wounds and lack of significant blood. Heart had already stopped bleeding." She looked at her notes. "A couple of other things. Expired driver's license shows this address." Espinoza took note that Warner was also breathing through her mouth which gave her a certain amount of comfort. "Oh, there was a business card for an Albuquerque attorney named Wilson Bennett in his pocket." Margaret was stunned. She knew Will Bennett well and wondered how the hell one of his business cards had gotten into the pocket of a dead guy in a drug house in the Valley.

"Given the nature of his teeth or lack thereof, he's probably a heavy meth user but we'll know more with the autopsy and toxicology."

Warner paused for effect. "We also found a part of an empty perfume bottle jammed up his rectum. Broken. The other part of the bottle was on the night stand and we have bagged it. May well be what cut him."

Chapter Two

The Investigation

Two of the detectives came back in the house and reported on their findings. There were the three out buildings on the property, the largest of which contained a rudimentary meth lab. It was clear to the detectives that, given the condition of the three survivors and the corpse, most of the profits from the operation were being consumed by the occupants of the house.

The second building was an outhouse that clearly had seen recent use given the smell of recent bowel movements and fresh toilet paper even though there was indoor plumbing or what passed for indoor plumbing inside. The third building was maybe 6 x 8 feet, the size of a garden shed. The door was open. And while it contained some basic tools like a rake and a shovel, what was weird about it was that it contained a soiled, filthy twin mattress on the floor.

Espinoza followed Detectives Bunker and Anderson out to the garden shed. In addition to the mattress, there were also a couple of shirts and a pair of pants, also filthy, and one pair of what used to be white jockey underwear.

Almost to herself, she said, "Is somebody living here?"

Both Bunker and Anderson shrugged. Bunker: "Hard to say. If the answer is 'yes', then whoever it is is living like an animal. Can't tell without more work when it was last used."

"Let's get a Crime Investigation Team out here, pronto. This is all getting a little too weird. We've got a dead guy with an "M" carved in his chest and a broken perfume bottle up his ass, three witnesses including the dead guy's brother who know nothing, a meth lab that looks like it's ready to blow up any time now, an outhouse that gets used regularly, and a garden shed that looks like somebody lives there. Oh, and no murder weapon. Really?"

"We're on it, Chief."

"Any neighbors hear anything?"

One of the uniformed officers stepped up.

"Chief, we're far enough south in the Valley that neighbors are at least a half mile away on each side of the property. Checked with both sides and nobody knew anything about the house or who lived in it. Or they know and don't want to be involved."

Margaret nodded. Either story was equally plausible.

The Homicide Chief cleared the area and headed downtown.

'OK, this truly is one of the strange ones.'

By the time she got back to headquarters, a lot of the preliminary background work had been done. In addition to Pablo and José Jiménez, the other two at the house were identified as Ricky Mendez and Juan Torres. All four were in their early to mid-twenties and all four had arrest records a mile long. Most were for drug related offenses and burglaries. José Jiménez had done time in the Penitentiary of New Mexico for assault with a deadly weapon and Juan Torres was in the same place at the same time for armed robbery. All carried prison or jail tattoos and all had some serious dental issues. The house itself was owned by Esther and Roberto Jiménez, the parents of the two brothers. The police were busy trying to find them.

She decided to start with the surviving brother who had been put in an interview room on the 4th Floor of Headquarters.

"I'm Detective Margaret Espinoza. Which one of you killed your brother?"

José Jiménez looked at her with a mixture of bravado and fear. He was sufficiently recovered from whatever he had been ingesting to know how serious the situation was. Skinny to the point of emaciation, a pock marked face, long greasy hair, clothes that reeked of body odor, and eyes too close to each other to be anything other than a fish, José was a wreck of a human being and, at least from Espinoza's perspective, had almost no redeemable human qualities whatsoever. He stared at her with those eyes too close together that were dark and beady and bright red all around the pupils.

"I don't know nothin,'" in heavily accented English. "Nothin'." Even from across the table, his breath was enough to make her gag. She took a deep breath – through her mouth.

"Mr. Jiménez, let me be perfectly straight up with you. The four of you have records out to here and all of you are looking at habitual offender status that is getting you back to PNM quicker than you can say 'I'm fucked.' You're running a meth lab on property your parents own, you've been holed up there for at least days, the blood screen we're running on you as we speak is going to light up like a Christmas tree. And your brother is deader than dead with a bullet hole in his brain you could drive a truck through. Don't you get it, asshole? This is the end of the line. Tell me what happened and maybe we can get some time off for you. Otherwise, you and your pals will never, ever see the light of day again."

They stared at each other for what seemed like forever. Finally, "I want a lawyer."

"We'll get you one, Mr. Jiménez, and you know what they're going to tell you? Just what I did." She got up never losing eye contact with him and left the room.

'Overwhelmed over the death of his brother,' she thought to herself as she walked away from his stench.

Interviews with the other two survivors didn't get much more. Ricky Mendez was no help at all, still not having recovered from the drug coma he'd put himself in back at the house. Juan Torres offered up that he and Ricky had crashed there a week ago and had been cranked up ever since. He had met José Jiménez at PNM and they had stayed in touch since they'd gotten out. He claimed to have no knowledge of how Pablo had gotten killed, never heard a gunshot, and knew nothing about the murder weapon. He finally wised up and shut up and asked for a lawyer. Detective Bunker walked out of the interview room with the same sense of nausea that the Chief of Homicide had had. Like Jiménez, Torres was emaciated, filthy, and tattooed over most of his body. Like Jiménez, he reeked of his filth. Charles Darwin would have been bitterly disappointed in the evolution of the species if this was the best that it could do.

Bunker, Anderson and Espinoza met in a conference room. At first glance it had seemed open and shut. There was an argument between the four, one of the surviving three bangers had killed Pablo and that was that. The trouble for the detectives was that when they began to pull the onion leaves back, it wasn't quite so simple. There was no gun, no motive other than an argument, no explanation for the "M" on the dead guy's chest, and for sure no reason why the killer would jam a broken part of an empty perfume bottle into the rectum of the dead guy. What the hell kind of symbolism was that? And so far they couldn't tell which of the surviving three had killed Pablo. She was certain it had to be one of them but proving which one wasn't going to be easy.

Espinoza had two thoughts. One, she wanted to listen to the original 911 tape that had the APD respond in the first place and, two, she wanted to talk to Will Bennett to find out why one of his business cards had been found on a dead banger in the South Valley.

The 911 tape was eerie:

Time: 9/13/17 1330 hours

DISPATCH: 911. "How may I help?

Long pause.

"DISPATCH: Hello, hello? 911. How can I help?

CALLER: *Hello? I would like to report loud noises.*

DISPATCH: What kind of noises, ma'am?

CALLER: *Not a ma'am.*

DISPATCH: I'm sorry, sir. What kind of noises?

CALLER: *Lots of noise. Maybe I heard a gunshot.*

DISPATCH: How long ago did you hear the gunshot?

CALLER: *I dunno. Maybe a few minutes ago.*

DISPATCH: How many minutes?

CALLER: *I dunno. But you better hurry.*

DISPATCH: Where?

CALLER: *1305 Desert Drive."*

Click.

The eerie part of it was the voice of the caller. English with a Hispanic accent but childlike almost. It was no wonder that the dispatcher thought she was talking to a woman. And to Espinoza, there was something else about the voice that she couldn't put her finger on. At least not at the moment. But it would come to her. It almost always did.

She left Anderson and Bunker, went across the street to get a Starbucks latte and settled in to think it through. She had gotten to know Will Bennett and his wife, Alex Kennedy, when she was investigating the murders of several of Will's partners at his law firm. Their paths crossed again when she was in charge of the investigation of the deaths of several courtroom employees and had crossed once more when she had been in charge of an unsuccessful investigation trying to track down the murderer of several men involved in a kickback construction scheme with state and federal government officials. Especially Alex had helped Margaret through the murder of her son and the three of them had become very close personal friends through it all and despite it all.

The receptionist at the law firm of Johnston & Blackwell, PLC answered the call and sent it directly to Will's phone. He recognized the main number of the APD, wondered vaguely what this could be about and picked up the phone.

"Will Bennett."

"Hey Will, it's Margaret Espinoza. How are you?"

'Oh geez, this can't be good.'

"Good, Margaret. You?"

"Fine, Will. Thanks for asking. Hey listen, your name, actually your business card, came up in a very strange place today and I wanted to follow up. You know a guy named Pablo Jiménez by any chance?"

Will searched his internal Rolodex and came up with nothing.

"Doesn't ring a bell off the top of my head. 'Sup?"

"We found him dead in a drug house in the South Valley this afternoon. Shot between the eyes. He had your business card in his jeans."

A pause that lasted to Will for what seemed like forever.

"Man, I have no idea. Let me run his name through our client base and see if anything turns up, OK?"

"Sounds good, Will. While you're at it why don't you also run the names of José Jiménez, Ricky Mendez, and Juan Torres? They were found at the house with the dead guy and we're assuming at least one of them is the shooter."

"Will do. I'll try to get back to you yet today."

"Sure thing."

He hung up the phone and took a deep breath. He really admired, liked and respected Margaret Espinoza but honestly every time she showed up in his life, people around him began to die. 'Course, the only reason she showed up was that somebody had already died. But still.

Margaret dialed the District Attorney's Office next, got an assistant on the line, explained what she had, and asked that the men be charged at least initially with felony murder. The

prosecutor had no questions and no objections. She called booking
next. The bangers were going nowhere soon.

Chapter Three

Will and Alex

Will found his assistant, Liz LaRue, at her desk and asked her to run the names through the firm's database. None of the names meant anything to Liz which meant there was about a 100% certainty that they wouldn't show up in any of the data banks. Certainly not the holiday card list given what Margaret Espinoza had told him.

Close enough to closing time, Will packed up a few things in his briefcase that he knew, and Liz knew, he'd never get to and headed to the elevator. On his way out, he looked around the office and thought how fortunate the fledging firm had been to find it. It was in downtown Albuquerque on Central Ave, built in the 19th Century, the fourth floor bought and rehabbed by a plaintiff's firm who had saved a lot of the brick and original wood, and, once done, promptly imploded and filed for bankruptcy. Johnston & Blackwell bought it from the bank that held the mortgage for a song in near turn key condition. Plus it was at most ten minutes from home.

For Will, home was a townhouse in Albuquerque's Old Town where he lived with two black cats, Jinks and Josie, and his wife, Alex Kennedy. The relationship between the two humans had gone much less smoothly than the relationships between the cats and the humans and there were so many times that one or the other would call it quits, that they had stopped counting. But there was something about the two of them that kept them coming back to each other, confounding not only themselves but everyone who knew them. It had been a long-distance affair for years with Alex practicing law in New Mexico and Will practicing law in Michigan.

Finally, Will had gotten to a place where his daughter, Grace, was off to college and there was little left to prove in Michigan. By then the Governor of New Mexico had had the rare good judgment of appointing Alex to the Second Judicial District Court bench and Will moved to Albuquerque, miraculously passed the Bar, and began practicing with a defense firm much like the one he'd left in Michigan.

He and Alex were married in a brief civil ceremony by a federal judge and finally found the peace and happiness they both needed and wanted. As they were quick to recognize, there would still be a few bumps in the road in the relationship and that had certainly been true but they survived almost against all odds. The old adage that marriage takes away the insecurity that makes relationships work had no application to the two of them. None whatsoever.

After a short time, he left the original firm and with several others started a law firm that was part plaintiff's personal injury work and part business law. The firm had survived the murders of several of its members, almost including Will himself, and, after that, prospered.

In the meantime, Alex was elected Chief Judge of the District and had herself survived the killings of several court employees as well as her own kidnapping and near death.

Will had just poured himself a neat Jameson Irish Whiskey, sat down in his favorite chair with the two cats on either side of him, when his cell rang. He got up, got to it on the last ring before voice mail, and recognized Liz's number.

"Hey, what's up?"

"Ran the names through the data base and the only thing close was a contact a little over a year ago by a middle aged couple named Roberto and Esther Jiménez. Pretty common name in these parts."

"Yep. What did they want -- can you tell?"

"Not really other than Jackie spent a few minutes with them and then referred them to one of the firms that does probate and guardian stuff."

"Can't imagine there's a connection but I guess I'll be a good citizen and pass it on. Contact information?"

"No phone. Address of an apartment complex in the near east side of the city." She gave the information to Will and they hung up. He looked at it for a minute, then found Margaret Espinoza's cell phone in his contacts and dialed her. It rang to voice mail and he left the message with the address of Esther and Robert Jiménez and never gave it another thought. For a while.

Chapter Four

Esther and Roberto Rodriguez

Two hours later when Margaret got the message, things began to escalate in the Jiménez murder investigation.

At right around 7 that evening, Detective Anderson and Chief Espinoza knocked on the door to Apartment 301 of the Desert Pines Apartments located about a mile and a half east of downtown. Nice apartments, in need of a little maintenance, but solidly middle class.

A Hispanic woman probably in her mid to late forties opened the door as far as the chain would allow.

"May I help you?"

"Are you Esther Jiménez?"

"I am. Who's asking?"

"Ma'am, my name is Margaret Espinoza and I'm a detective with the Albuquerque Police Department. This is Detective Anderson." They both showed her their badges. "May we come in? It's about your sons, Pablo and José."

They both saw her face drop and tears well up. She turned away from the opening in the door and yelled into the interior, "Roberto, the police are here. It's about the boys." She shut the door enough to release the chain and let them in.

The apartment was immaculately clean and all Margaret could think of was the mess they had seen that afternoon. Roberto Jiménez was a handsome man, maybe 5'8" tall, in his forties or early fifties, trim and fit. He had salt and pepper hair, a well lined brown face, brown eyes, and a well-manicured moustache. His wife was a petite woman, younger by a few years than her husband, and still very attractive.

The two detectives sat down on the couch and confirmed that Pablo and José were their sons.

"I am so sorry to have to tell you this but your son, Pablo, was killed this afternoon at a house on Desert Drive." She waited for the universally common reaction of grief and shock but, to her surprise, there was none of that, just blank stares back at her from both of them. Off her game for a minute, Margaret hurried on, "He was shot and there were some other men in the house, including your son, José. We're holding all three of them in custody as 'persons of interest'." Again nothing, and for the longest moment, the four adults in the room just stared at each other in uncomfortable silence.

Finally, Detective Anderson broke the ice. "We're sorry to be bringing you this bad news, but we do have some questions for the two of you."

Husband and wife stared at him.

"Our understanding is that the house where it happened is titled in your names. Is that true?"

It was Roberto Jiménez who finally broke the silence.

"Yes, we have owned it for several years."

"And did you live there?"

"Yes, until about three years ago." He thought for a moment, seemed to make up his mind about something, and then offered this, "We tried to raise the boys right and did everything we could. But they wouldn't stay in school and started hanging out with the wrong people in the Valley and almost every day it seemed like one or the other was in trouble. Lots of violence, lots of drugs. Prison time, jail time. Finally, Esther couldn't take it anymore, we told the boys the house was theirs, we never wanted to see them again and we moved here." His arm swept the apartment. "They never tried to contact us and we never tried to contact them. But I will tell you this, it's no surprise that one of them is dead. I guess the only surprise is that they have lasted this long."

"When the police arrived this afternoon, three of the men were in the living room clearly under the influence of drugs." She saw both of them nod. "Pablo was in the bedroom. Do you think José could have killed his brother?" Both of them shrugged their shoulders in unison.

"They were animals, Detective. No telling what they'd do to each other or anybody else."

"The other two men who were there were Ricky Mendez and Juan Torres. Ring any bells?" They both shook their heads again in unison.

"When was the last time you were at the house?"

They looked at each other and Esther said, "Right around three years ago, when we left for the last time and moved here. We never wanted to see it again. We took some retirement and paid off the mortgage and paid the taxes to keep it current but that's all."

Margaret thought about the "M" carved on their son's chest and the meth lab in the out building but it was clear that there would be no more answers to any of those questions. The two detectives asked a few more background questions – both of them were employed in factory jobs, no debt, just simple folks making their way in the world with the tragedy of two out of control sons to always be a cloud over them.

The detectives got up to leave and as they got to the door and opened it, Margaret turned and asked, "There's a garden shed on the property and it looks as though somebody may have been living in it. Know anything about that?" Both detectives noticed a flicker of the eyes in both of them. "We don't know anything, Detective. Sorry." And politely but firmly closed the door.

Anderson and Espinoza looked at each other. Both had seen it.

"Somethin' there," said Anderson.

"Yep."

"Something else. No family pictures anywhere in the apartment, not even of just the two of them."

"Yep."

Chapter Five

More Questions than Answers

The next day, the detective team in charge of the investigation began to get some answers which did nothing more than raise more questions.

First of all, they met with the Crime Investigation Unit members that had gone over the property. The meth lab was crude and amateurish and the CIU team announced that had meth continued to be produced there, it was only a short time before it, and everything in it, would have blown sky high. That confirmed what Margaret already knew. The outhouse had been used within 24 to 48 hours before the team hit the property given an analysis of the waste they found. Same was true of the garden shed – somebody had been there within 24 to 48 hours ahead of the CIU people according to an analysis of the bedding. There was evidence of dried semen on the sheets that couldn't be dated but they would run the DNA. The drugs in the house were identified as very poor quality meth and the likely source was the outbuilding. The detectives had been right the day before – the bangers were using their own product.   What was most remarkable was what the team didn't find. There was no evidence of any gun on the premises. They confirmed what the ME had opined at the scene. The broken piece of the perfume bottle was used to carve the "M" on the chest. But there was nothing to explain the symbolism of either the "M" or the perfume bottle in the rectum. Many, many sets of fingerprints most of which belonged to the four bangers but some other random ones as well.

Early afternoon, Margaret got a call from Dr. Steven Kessler, the pathologist in charge of the Jiménez autopsy.

"Cause of death was the gunshot to the head. Hollow point .45 that did a lot of damage and never came out. In addition, lots of damage to the brain from drugs. What was left after the hollow point got done looked more like Swiss cheese than brain tissue." Margaret winced. "In terms of the cutting, I agree with ME Warner that it came after he was dead. Done with the perfume bottle. Any idea why "M"?

"None."

"Still too soon for toxicology back from the lab but it's certain it will show major drugs on board at the time of his death."

"How close was the gun to the head?"

"Good question. Close. Powder burns around the entrance wound."

"So he must have known the individual?"

"Well, if it was one of the three who killed him, then of course. On the other hand, if it was a stranger, Pablo might well have been completely out of it, laid down on the bed to sleep it off, and got killed that way."

Margaret thought about that for a minute. She had been working under the assumption that one of the three in the house had pulled the trigger. But Kessler raised the possibility of somebody coming in the house, shooting Pablo, carving him up, getting rid of a perfume bottle in a very strange place, and then leaving. It would explain the lack of a gun at the scene.

She made a note to have CIU run the rest of the prints through the system to see if there was some other kind of match. And to check the make of the perfume and where it could be purchased in the greater Albuquerque area.

On the other hand, she had Mendez, Torres, and Jiménez on about seven dozen felony murder counts and, in some ways, it didn't matter who pulled the trigger. One or all of them were going down for it. Unless it was a third party. And where was the goddamned gun? It wasn't like the three bangers were in particularly good shape when the cops got there, certainly not good enough shape to shoot a man and then hide the murder weapon so nobody could find it. And what's the deal with the garden shed and the outhouse? Jesus.

Then Margaret Espinoza smiled to herself. This is what she loved, it's what got her over her son's death, and it's what got her up every day to a new dawn. She'd figure it out, she knew it.

Chapter Six

Michigan in the Fall

Alex and Will took a few days away from the craziness of their lives and got back to the lake house in West Michigan in late September. It had been an early fall and the leaves were at their best – golds and reds and yellows. Coupled with sunny but cool weather, it was perfect for the two of them. After their latest crisis involving Alex reengaging in a relationship that had gone on long before Will had entered the picture and after somehow coming back around the bend from that, the two of them had pledged to try to make time for each other.

Getting back to Will's roots was one way to do it. He had kept the house even after he had permanently moved to New Mexico. His daughter, Grace, was still in West Michigan and used it a lot and had made her dad promise he wouldn't sell it unless it was between dog food for dinner and keeping the house in which case she would reluctantly agree he could put it on the market. Plus, in what seemed like so many years before, his best friend had died in the house and Will felt a special kinship with Sam's spirit when he was there. And finally, Alex had grown to love it there as well as long as it wasn't winter. So it stayed in the family.

They flew Southwest into Grand Rapids, rented a car, bought enough groceries and Irish Whiskey to get them by, and got to the lake house to find it ready and warm. Their neighbor, Rusty Rhoades, had come over and turned the heat and water on and, once Will got a fire in the wood stove, life was good. The view of Lake Michigan in all her splendor never failed to move Will and Alex felt the same way. They stayed up just long enough to see the sun set and then, even with the time change, they went to bed and slept and slept and slept. Until there was a knock at the door.

"Hey brothers and sisters, thought you might be in the mood for a walk on the beach! 'Sup, folks?"

Will loved Rusty and he had been a friend to Will when Will was down to a precious few of them. But seriously? Pounding on the door for a walk in the middle of the night? Seriously? And then they both figured it out. It was 9 AM in Michigan and the sun was up. It was 7 AM in New Mexico and still dark.

"Oops. Sorry. Sorry." Rusty began to do his best imitation of a moon walk backward out the door.

"Do your walk and come back for coffee. I'll try to have some underwear on by then. Maybe Alex too." He watched his friend walk away and marveled again at the friendship that had endured through so much. A man's man, master carpenter, master woodsman and fisherman, master of his universe, it was only after getting to know him that you got the real Rusty. Well read, far more sensitive than he let on, and a Lutheran faith that had sustained him and his forbears for decades in the same community. An American treasure.

Will went back to bed and found Alex up and reading her phone. She put it down and looked at him, "How long before he's back?"

"45 minutes at the earliest. Have something in mind?"

"Let's see if we can get this plane landed, cowboy." He felt her hands began to move.

Afterwards when he was making coffee, Will wondered about the freshness of it all. Sure they had slowed down some and sure there had been those bumps in the road along the way but she still was the magic for him and hopefully him for her. She was one of those women who got better looking with age and the lines and wrinkles and crinkles were all hard fought and well deserved. She kept her hair short and professional with a few highlights just to make her feel better about herself although she knew it was pure vanity. After the recent separation that had lasted some months, both had come back to each other a little better tuned physically and they kept to the promise to keep as fit as they could especially with a life style that was sedentary and stressful. So far, they were holding steady. He took the two cups of coffee back to the bedroom.

Rusty got back in less than an hour and the three of them took the time to get caught up. Business as a contractor/carpenter was better than ever and that was a constant source of tension for his friend because every job he took meant another day he couldn't be in the woods or on the water. Will at one point in their friendship had pointed out that jobs that paid well also paid for gas in the boat, lures for the fish, arrows for the cross bow, and bullets for the rifle but it was a hard sell. Fish fry Friday for Rusty's family and friends, Will and Alex, and Will's daughter, Grace.

On his way out, Rusty told them, "Here's an idea. If you're not doing anything today, why don't the two of you take your boat out and see if you can scare up some fish to contribute for tomorrow night."

After he left, Will and Alex looked at each other.

Alex, who was born and raised and lived her life in New Mexico and who had once been in a row boat at the state fair, had never been a huge fan of boats but it was a beautiful day, the sun would warm things up, the color in the trees was at its spectacular best, and they would be together. What could go wrong?

As it turns out…

They made some sandwiches and packed some soda and beer, got the boat that Will kept in the storage shed hooked up to the Jeep they kept at the lake house, and were ready to go. Two things should have happened that didn't. One, Will should have checked the gas tank on the boat to make sure there was enough and, two, he should have checked the charge on the batteries to make sure there was enough to get the boat started.

They went to the lake that had the largest launch in the area and that gave Will the best chance to get the boat in the water without hitting something like another boat or someone like an innocent bystander. Unfortunately, Will was a little out of practice in terms of backing the boat up and it took several times to get it straight enough to get the trailer in the water. The patience of the six boaters who were waiting for him was, at best, wearing thin. Plus Will figured they were all carrying and someone was likely to pull a gun out to hurry things along. Talk about performance anxiety. So Will finally got the boat in the water, thought it was in deep enough to pull the trailer out and have Alex hold the line when he realized he'd forgotten to remove the lines holding the boat on the trailer. The boat would never leave the trailer.

The crowd at the top of the ramp began to look more like vigilantes than fishermen. Will calmly pulled the trailer and boat back up, undid the straps, and backed back down. This time they were successful getting it off the trailer and Alex held the line while Will got the Jeep and trailer away from the launch and parked. Back down to the launch, they both got into the boat, got the motor down, and tried to get it started. A couple of anemic attempts right at the launch were unsuccessful and they decided to let it float out a bit to avoid what clearly was now a mob scene at the launch. Twenty minutes later, the motor finally caught and they both congratulated themselves on their success.

Will got the boat as far away from the launch ramp as he could as quickly as he could only to have the motor sputter and finally die altogether. He tried various things to get it started until Alex finally asked whether there was gas in the container. There was not. Alex suggested they ask one of the power boats on the water to tow them in, a suggestion that fell on Will's deaf ears. 'These guys want to hang me for taking so much time and now I need their help? I don't think so.'

So, they began the arduous task of rowing back in to the launch ramp. Two hours later, they were close enough to appreciate that the mob had all gotten their boats launched and the area was empty. Unfortunately, the attempt to get the boat back on the trailer was complicated by Will's inability to once again back the trailer in the water without a half dozen trailer jack knifes. Then while they were getting the boat centered on the trailer, both of them fell into the cool – but not frozen – water.

Wet and tired, they got in the Jeep and pulled the boat out far enough to get it battened down and got on their way.

She just couldn't help herself, "You know for a fisherman, you're a pretty good lawyer."

In another time, he might have taken the bait but he kept his thoughts to himself. Why? Because speaking of bait, he'd also forgotten to get any. It started with a smile, then a giggle, then full blown hysterical laughter that lasted damn near all the way back to the lake house.

It was midafternoon before all was said and done and the boat put away and they collapsed in the lounge chairs on the deck in the warmth of the afternoon sun.

"You still love me, Alex?"

"Somebody has to, Will."

"Nap?"

"Sure."

Ninety minutes later, they woke up with the nightmare of the day in the boat almost behind them. They went early to the Inn for some perch, had a couple of drinks, and were sort of dreamy eyed about each other. The Inn was a tradition not because of the quality of the food but because of the ambience. In the 19th Century, it had been a trading post for the white men who had descended on West Michigan for the prized White Pines that they could lumber and then ship out for building materials back east. For as long as Will had owned the lake house, it had been the locals' favorite restaurant.

In large part, in all candor, because the bartenders had a heavy hand with the pour and that more than made up for any issues with the menu.

During the course of the meal, Alex filled Will in on the dinner she had had with Margaret Espinoza two nights before they left for Michigan. Margaret had told her about this very strange homicide case she was working on involving meth addicts, lost murder weapons, chest carvings, and perfume bottles. And that triggered his conversation with Margaret about the cops having found Will's business card in the dead guy's pocket which had totally slipped his mind until this very moment. Strange coincidences all around.

"Let's get back for the sunset, Will."

They got in the jeep and were about half way home when Alex's cell phone rang. Another coincidence. It was Margaret Espinoza.

"Is Will with you, Alex?" No hello, how are you, just 'is Will with you?'

"Yep, he's right here."

"May I talk to him?" Certainly had her cop voice in gear. She handed the phone to Will.

"Hey, Margaret."

"Hey, Will. I've got some bad news. You remember me calling you about your card in the pocket of the Jiménez kid and me asking you to run him through your data bank?"

"I do."

"You came up with Esther and Roberto Jiménez with an address for them. Turns out they owned the house where the murder took place and were the parents of Pablo and José."

'Were? Oh, this can't be good.'

"They're dead, Will. Probably murder/suicide."

Chapter Seven

Reality

Alex had heard both sides of the conversation and they drove the rest of the way back to the lake house each lost in their thoughts. Will remembered what Liz had told him about the contact with the firm a while ago and that Jackie had referred it out. Will apparently had never met the people. Now they were dead and his business card had been found on their son's body. Great.

Margaret had suggested they come back at their earliest convenience and both struggled with having to miss the fish fry and the opportunity to see Grace. Fortunately, the airplane gods intervened. There were no flights out of Grand Rapids to Albuquerque on Friday.

And so the next day dawned as beautiful as the day before with sun and warmer temperatures. Will and Alex took a long walk in the woods holding hands and marveling at the wonder of the changing of the seasons. Will especially loved the fall – it always brought a sense of nostalgia of friends and family gone by and the walk in the woods with the smell of the leaves in the forest was beyond ambrosia. He was a happy guy with the small niggle bothering him of what was going on back in Albuquerque. He really didn't see how it affected him or the firm much; there had been an incidental contact and the Jiménez couple had been referred out. When he got back he would check with Jackie and see if they could track down what firms the couple had been referred to.

Friday night was a blast. Grace had brought a date, a nice young architect named Jack, who seemed to fit in well with the mix. Even Will liked him which was a true miracle at least in the eyes of his daughter and wife. Alex had learned early on that as much as she knew Will loved her, Grace was always No. 1 in his heart. They had been close their entire lives and, even with the geographic distance between them, they were still close, texting, emailing, or even, God forbid, talking on the phone several times a week. Grace had become the permanent law clerk of an Article III federal district court judge and was the judge's primary 'go to' person on complicated matters. She had been through a lot in her young life and seeing her glow with happiness meant the world to Will.

The fish were terrific, the potato salad to die for, and the company even better, and when they finally got back to the lake house, Jack and Grace had a glass of wine and Alex and Will some Jameson. They sat on the deck and marveled at the stars, so brilliantly white against the dark sky. Small talk about life and jobs and both catching up and getting to know Jack a little better in the smaller crowd. The original plan had been for Jack and Grace to stay the weekend with the old folks but Alex had gotten them on a flight back to New Mexico first thing Saturday so the two youngsters would have it to themselves at least for part of the time. If he was being honest, it made Will a little uncomfortable knowing his daughter was sleeping in the same bed as her boyfriend but what the hell, she was 28 years old and certainly more mature at her age than he had ever been in his entire life. What he didn't and couldn't know was that Jack was just as uncomfortable with the arrangement as Will was and breathed a sigh of relief when he realized Will and Alex were leaving the next day.

That day came earlier than anybody wanted it to and there was some regret about the amount of alcohol consumed the night before but a couple of Tylenol and some good coffee got things straightened out. They said their goodbyes with Will once again for maybe the millionth time reminding Grace to turn the pump and the water heater off when they left. If only he could have seen the eye roll.

Normally traveling with Alex was a joy because they had each other's undivided attention for a block of time but this time Will was a little out of sorts. He couldn't quite put his hands on exactly why but his office had somehow touched some lives that were now gone forever. He had no idea why he was feeling some responsibility for it but there it was.

It would get much, much worse.

On Monday morning, Will met Margaret Espinoza at Garcia's on Central. Everybody thought it best that the judge stay out of any discussions having to do with an ongoing murder investigation. Although she didn't have to, Margaret filled Will in on the deaths of the Jiménez parents. Apparently, no one had seen them coming and going for several days so one of the neighbors knocked and when there was no answer, the manager had been called and unlocked the door. He found Esther and Roberto in bed together both with gunshots to the temple and with the weapon in Esther's hand. The Medical Examiner, the police, and the prosecutor all called it murder/suicide and the case seemed open and shut. There had been no suicide note which was frustrating as hell and Margaret clearly felt responsibility for being the one to tell them the news about their sons especially given what she had been through with her own son. But it was what it was. The boys, by any stretch, weren't exactly model citizens even in their parents' eyes.

Will told her he would get with Jackie as soon as he got to the office and would call her first thing.

"I'm still struggling with how your business card got in Pablo's pocket, Will. Any thoughts?"

Actually, he had thought a lot about it since she had told him but there really wasn't a good answer. The only place the couple had been was in the reception area of the firm. He never carried them in his wallet and couldn't remember the last time he'd given one to anybody other than a client. Even if Roberto and Esther had picked one up when they were there, that was over a year ago and they had told Margaret they hadn't see their sons in several years. So one more mystery for which there was no good answer.

"Unless one or both of them were seeing the boys more than they were letting on." Almost to herself. "And following that line of inquiry, one of them could have gotten the business card and given it to one or both of their sons if they ever needed a lawyer."

"But why me? I don't do criminal work at all. Seems like the more likely business card would be the Public Defender, wouldn't you think?"

"Honestly, I don't know what to think." At his request, she gave him her check. "Thanks for breakfast, Will. You've always supported APD's finest. Call me when you talk to Jackie."

On her way to the office, she called CIU, had them confirm fingerprints for both Roberto and Esther and run them by what they were finding at 1305 Desert Drive. Next, she called her office and had them prepare a search warrant for Apt. 301. She was still looking for the gun.

Will Bennett got to the offices of Johnston & Blackwell, PLC, got a cup of coffee and went looking for Liz and Jackie LaPointe. Jackie was the newest lawyer in the firm having just graduated from the University of New Mexico Law School *magna cum laude* but she had been a member of the firm from the beginning. Starting as a gopher, she had worked her way to IT guru, then to office manager, then to law clerk, and now an associate. She was a rock star and very close not just to Alex and Will but to everybody in the firm. She had started with lots of tattoos and piercings but as time had gone on, she had lost most of them as discretionary money became available. She had married the love of her life who had completed an anesthesiology residency and who was now on staff at UNM Hospital.

He found the two of them in the breakroom and they sat down at one of the tables. Liz had filled Jackie in on what they were looking for and Jackie had a vague recollection of her meeting with the couple. They had come to Johnston & Blackwell because of the publicity surrounding a trial that Will and Rosalind McManus had had representing the Ruiz family who had lost their husband and father in a construction accident. The verdict was for $18,000,000 which can, to say the least, attract notice for someone who just might be looking for a lawyer. The firm had been inundated with calls after the verdict and Mr. and Mrs. Jiménez had made an appointment that ended up on Jackie's calendar.

"Honestly, I don't remember much about them, Will, other than they came in to see about a guardianship or conservatorship or something for one of their sons. I told them we didn't handle stuff like that and gave them the names of the Arenas firm and the Richardson firm both of whom do that kind of work. I remember them being very appreciative especially when I told them there was no charge for the initial consultation. That's the last I heard of them until this morning."

"How did they get into the data bank?"

Liz: "I always run any person that comes in to see us to see whether we take the case or not."

Will nodded. 'Good practice. Wonder why I never knew that.'

They exchanged pleasantries and caught up with what was going on at the office since Will and Alex had been in Michigan and then split up to get on with the day. Will called Margaret Espinoza and filled her in on the discussion with Jackie. She said she would follow up with the firms and thanked him again for breakfast.

"Keep me posted if there's anything else you need, Margaret." Regretting it as soon as he said it.

Chapter Eight

More Questions Than Answers, Part II

The next several days flew by for Will as they always did. There were a number of good plaintiffs' cases in the pipeline still in large part left over from the Ruiz verdict and Rosalind, Luis Moreno, Jackie, and Will were working them up through the discovery slog. Lots of written questions to be answered by the clients, lots of written statements under oath to be taken, and experts to be contacted and retained.

Johnston & Blackwell, PLC was a bit of a hybrid firm because it contained both business lawyers and trial lawyers. Generally, those two groups tended not to play well together because of the difference in personalities between the two and because business lawyers were paid by the hour and personal injury plaintiffs' attorneys were paid on a percentage of what the verdict or settlement might be in any given case. If they lost, they got nothing and usually had spent gobs of money that, in almost all cases, they wouldn't recoup. That made business lawyers very nervous to say the least. Plus at least Will always thought trial lawyers were a lot more fun, a viewpoint he shared with no one other than Alex who before being appointed to the bench had had a very successful run as a plaintiff's attorney. She agreed.

Nevertheless, the firm prospered because of the personalities of the lawyers and staff. They were not only colleagues but also good friends and it made it fun to go to work in the morning. Morton Blackwell was the head business lawyer and was not only a very good lawyer but also well connected politically because his father-in-law was the former mayor of Albuquerque. Luis Moreno was also a very good trial lawyer and had miraculously recovered from a serious heart ailment that had caused Will Bennett to return to the practice of law from a construction job in Michigan to try the Ruiz case. To this day, Luis swore on his mother's grave that he truly had been at death's door but as the weeks and months went by and Luis was operating at full speed without let up, even the most naïve of colleagues had to question the diagnosis.

It also helped the collegiality of Johnston & Blackwell that the Ruiz case had settled while the case was on appeal and a very sizeable fee was added to the firm's coffers, thanks to the team who had tried the case.

Meanwhile, Judge Kennedy likewise was busier than ever although there was a frustration to her job that was beginning to wear thin. The problem? Nobody ever tried cases anymore and trials especially with good trial lawyers were the most fun for judges. She had read recently that nationwide, only about 1% to 2% of the civil cases like personal injury lawsuits actually went to trial and only about 3% of criminal cases went to trial because there were so many plea deals cut. So that meant judges like Alex spent most of their time handling pretrials, resolving petty disputes among litigants who should grow up and be adults, administrating stuff especially as the Chief Judge, hearing endless motions on Zoo Day which is what everybody called the day when motions were heard, and writing opinions on matters that damn near bored her to tears. She and Will had talked about her retiring and maybe joining the firm in some capacity or another. Alex yearned to be back in the courtroom trying cases again although if only 1% to 2% went to trial she would end up like Will being mostly a Get Ready for Trial Lawyer instead of a Trial Lawyer. Plus she knew trial work was a young person's game and, in her mid fifties just three years younger than Will, she wasn't getting any younger.

She still had lots of energy and knew she could do it in the short term but long term it would take its toll. She could see it in Will. So she buckled down for another round of deciding petty disputes by petty lawyers and, in her mind, womaned up.

Across the way at Police Headquarters, a monolithic five story concrete building that looked exactly like a police headquarters should, information continued to dribble in on the Jiménez murder. It was not the hot button these days for Chief of Homicide Espinosa because the statistics showed that most homicides are solved in the first days after the murder; the more the time passed, the less chance there was for success. And God knows there were plenty of recent homicides in Albuquerque to keep her team hopping. Besides, she continued to think she had a lock on felony murder on all three of the bangers unless there was some shadow killer out there and, regardless, the three were going nowhere except to PNM for a very long time. Plus the dead guy could hardly be called a pillar of the community so what did it matter?

Then two things rocked her. One, CIU advised her that they had found fingerprints at the Desert Drive home that matched those of Esther Jiménez and while that wasn't particularly conclusive because the couple had lived there for a number of years before moving out and leaving it their sons, it was odd. Two, the gun used in the murder/suicide pact matched the ballistics of the gun that killed Pablo – it was the same gun. Had Esther Jiménez gone to 1305 Desert Drive and killed one of her sons? Without anybody else seeing or hearing her? That seemed so far-fetched as to be laughable. But how did the murder weapon end up in the murder/suicide? Or was it a murder/suicide or just murder? So then who's the killer? José Jiménez is in jail as are Ricky

Mendez and Juan Torres so rule them out. Who else could there be?

She called CIU back and had them go back to Apt. 301 this time looking for any evidence of foul play. She next made a call to Esther's employer to confirm she was working on the day her son was killed and the answer was in the affirmative – day shift so she couldn't have been the one to pull the trigger. She went to get a latte. She was missing something, she just didn't know what.

The Jiménez murder just got back on the front burner.

Chapter Nine

Perfume

Dr. Kessler called the next morning.

"We analyzed the perfume from the bottle in the rectum. Something called *Vanilla Mist for Women.*"

"Tell me there's only one store in Albuquerque that carries it and the store keeps track of anybody who buys a bottle."

"Wish I could, Detective, but that would make your job way too easy. I had one of my assistants check around and apparently you can pretty much buy it at any discount or chain store you go to. Costs about ten bucks. Not found in fine stores anywhere but a pretty good seller because of the price. This one is not likely to go on the Christmas list for Mrs. Kessler this year."

"All right. Thanks for following through on this."

"Quite all right. Oh, and one other thing. It was most likely broken after the decedent was shot and then half of it was used to carve the "M." The other half, as you know, ended up in his rectum for reasons that escape me – and, as you know, this ain't my first rodeo. One other thing I can tell you. Whoever the killer, there seems to be a fair amount of rage built into this one. Talk to you later."

Margaret hung up the phone and pondered it all again. This wasn't getting any easier.

Chapter Ten

Ricky Mendez

That afternoon, Margaret got a call from J.D Rawlings, the prosecutor in charge of the Pablo Jiménez murder.

"Ricky Mendez wants to make a deal so says his Public Defender, Ginny Beckwith."

"What's he got to sell that's worth anything? He's the one who was in a coma when the cops got there."

"Not much probably but he's got the most to lose on felony murder because he has the least numbers on his rap sheet and the least violent. Might be worth shaving a few years if he's got something that's helpful."

"Settin' up a meeting?"

"Yep. Tomorrow morning at 9. Can you make it?"

"Sure. Where?"

"Bernalillo County Jail. Be there be square."

The next morning, Rawlings and Espinoza and Beckwith and Mendez met in an interview room at the jail. The jail had moved from downtown to out west of Albuquerque a few years back because of overcrowding and difficulty keeping order in the packed house. Now the new jail was overcrowded and there was difficulty keeping order in the packed house. Another thing that hadn't changed were the smells of the jail house and the interview room reeked of old body odors, urine, and something else Margaret couldn't and didn't want to identify. She was breathing through her mouth – again.

"My client is willing to give a complete statement of what he knows in exchange for a plea deal that will give him no jail or prison time," Beckwith puffed up with the arrogance of a newbie PD.

Rawlings got up to leave. "That will never happen. What a waste. C'mon, Detective."

"Wait." Mendez talking this time. "I'll tell you what I know."

Of the four at the scene of the murder, he was in the best condition physically. About 5'10" and a solid 180 pounds, he could be called handsome by some save for the tattoos on his neck and cheek, and two missing front teeth. His hair was coal black and eyes bright blue and Espinoza's first thought was that he wouldn't do well at PNM looking that good.

"Guess I could recommend a plea to Accessory to Murder which would get you maybe five to eight at PNM. That's probably the best I could do and get it past the judge. It depends a lot on what you know."

Beckwith asked to be alone with her client for a few minutes and came out after a bit and said Mendez had agreed to give a statement on that "promise" by Rawlings.

A court reporter was summoned and the two hour statement with Rawlings, Espinoza, Mendez and Beckwith got under way.

On her way back to Albuquerque, she mulled over what they had learned. Mendez and Torres had gotten to Desert Drive five days before Jiménez was killed.

The four men had known each other since childhood ('then why didn't parents recognize the names?') and had been involved in gangs and small-time crimes most of their adolescent and early adult lives. They worked when they had to and also lived off what they could steal and what relatives or girlfriends would give them. None of them had gotten past 8th grade and all had done jail time. Mendez told them that Torres had also had a stint at PNM which is where he met up again with José Jiménez. After the two of them had gotten out of prison, they all had stayed in touch, hung out together, peddled some drugs, and tried to stay out of trouble long enough to get off parole. It wasn't easy because that's the only thing any of them were any good at – getting in trouble – and they weren't very good at that either.

While Torres was in prison, Mendez claimed he tried to clean up his act. He got a job at a Chick-fil-A as a server but that only lasted one shift as it became abundantly clear he not only couldn't get orders right, he couldn't make change. The manager gave him a break and put him on clean up duty which meant he hung around his shift, kept the bathrooms clean, and swept up after hours. His undoing came three days later when a toilet he was trying to unplug had other ideas and began spewing some very bad waste into the women's bathroom that quickly seeped out into the main area of the restaurant. They had to close the place for three days until the Health Department gave the OK to reopen but unfortunately that kind of publicity doesn't bode well for future business. Mendez was out of the first job he had held for more than a few hours. He tried a couple of other minimum wage jobs but lack of education, lack of motivation, and, frankly, a complete lack of common sense doomed him as well.

He was living on the streets when Juan Torres got out of prison and they quickly hooked up together again doing what they could to survive. Mendez reconnected with José Jiménez on a couple of occasions when he would hang around with Torres. His impression was the same as it had always been - that José was a tough guy and not somebody to mess with. So he kept his distance as best he could. Or so he said.

Then Jiménez had called Torres and told him to get Mendez and get to the Desert Valley address for "good times, man." Against Mendez's better judgment – which the detective thought was a stretch that Mendez had any judgment, much less better judgment – Mendez went along. That started a five-day binge of twenty four hour meth use mixed in with some very bad cocaine and some better than average marijuana – plus some beer, plus some Crown Royal. Mendez remembered bits and pieces but there were some very large gaps in his recollection. He knew the meth was homemade but didn't have the curiosity or the courage to see the operation first hand.

The most interesting part of the statement had to do with his knowledge of the garden shed. From time to time, either Pablo and José would go out to the shed and stay, as best as Mendez could put it together later, for anywhere from hours to overnight. Never at the same time. In his fog, Mendez couldn't figure it out because, as far as he knew, all the good stuff was in the house. He meant to ask what they were doing out there but his mind lost its thread and he never got back to it.

He had no recollection of the day Pablo was killed and thinks he was passed out the entire day. In fact, his first recollection of anything that day was being booked for felony murder. It was the first he knew somebody had died. Mendez was quick to point out that the entire time he was there, he saw no weapons whatsoever. And no, he never remembered anyone, man or woman, who was at the house other than the four of them.

At the end of the statement, Rawlings expressed disappointment at the quality and quantity of Ricky's recollection but said they would see what he could do on a plea deal. Ginny Beckwith asked if there were anyway Mendez could get out on bail.

"No way, Ginny. For all three of these guys, bail will be in the hundreds of thousands of dollars and no bail bondsman in his right mind would take a chance with any of these guys. No way."

"Never hurts to ask, Mr. Rawlings."

"Never hurts, Ms. Beckwith."

He walked to the parking lot with Margaret.

"What'd you think?"

"Not very useful, I guess, although the garden shed thing is a bubble off plumb. Wonder what they were doing?"

"Of the two people who know, one's dead and one isn't talking – about anything."

"If he's right about no weapons – and who knows if he's right – then the murder weapon would have had to have come in with a third party and left the same way. Right?"

"I guess so, Margaret, but do we really make either Esther or Roberto Jiménez coming out to the old homestead with a .45, culling Pablo from the herd, killing him point blank between the eyes, then carving a "M" on his chest, then sticking a perfume bottle up his ass? Yuk. If one of them had that kind of rage, why not just kill them all? Wasn't like they were in really good shape to defend themselves."

"I know, J.D., I know."

On the way back to town, Margaret got a call from CIU reporting that they had found nothing to indicate the apartment was anything but a place where a murder/suicide had taken place.

She called Dr. Kessler at the morgue and asked about the autopsies of Esther and Roberto Jiménez. For the most part, he said it was routine – cause of death in each was a bullet hole to the temple cause by a .45 – but there were a couple of oddities. Roberto had some bruising on one arm that went around most of his left wrist. There are lots of ways to get bruises in life but Kessler said he could make an argument that a hand had done that. The other oddity was a stunner – the gun was found in Esther's right hand consistent with a bullet wound to the right temple. Esther Jiménez was left handed.

Margaret Espinoza felt a headache coming on.

Chapter Eleven

Margaret

Two days later, Margaret was no further ahead on the Jiménez investigation but was plenty busy with a multiple homicide on the east side of Albuquerque in which two prostitutes and a pimp were killed by a man wielding an assault weapon. As they were piecing it together, it looked like a shake down with a "john" that went very badly. The problem now was finding the shooter and they weren't getting anywhere. The press didn't like it and neither did Margaret.

But that night, for the first time in forever, she had an honest to God date with a man. J.D. Rawlings had called the afternoon of the Mendez interview and had asked her to dinner. She almost defaulted to her "I'm busy" but for whatever reason said yes. She had worked with J.D. on a number of cases, liked his no bull shit no politics style, and liked the way he backed the cops when he could. Plus he wasn't bad on the eyes – tall and rangy with a cowboy look to him, sandy hair, a scar above one eye that there had to be a story about, and a smile and a warmth that had won him a lot of convictions in front of a lot of juries.

Margaret Espinoza had never spent much time thinking about her appearance as she was making her way up the ladder of the Albuquerque Police Department but she was no slouch in the looks department. Good Hispanic genes had given her a brown, almost unlined face, dark hair that she touched up from time to time, and eyes that could drill a hole in a criminal. Average height, she worked out endlessly at the police gym and was in great shape, a trait that was helpful in the kind of jobs she had held and was holding now. She had run down many a slow-footed defendant, tackled them, and had them in handcuffs before they knew she was a woman.

She had avoided pretty much any social life at all in furtherance of her career and in being the best single mother she could be to her son, Ronnie. He had been the product of a very short term relationship that had ended the night she told the guy she was pregnant. He had excused himself, picked up his jacket from her dining room chair, and walked out. She never saw him again. She raised her son with the best values she knew and she had family and friends who had her back. It wasn't as though she wasn't interested in men, it was just that there seemed to be so little time for the frivolity of dating. Plus, if she were honest, dating a woman who wore a uniform and carried a gun had a certain dampening effect on most men's ardor. Then her son was killed by an insane man and life stopped for a long time. Without Ronnie, there truly was nothing to live for and the friends and family that had been with her through thick and thin couldn't get her out of the darkness. Interestingly, it was a case she never solved that gave her back a spark of life that now, every day, got a little brighter. Shortly after a trial in which Will and his firm won the verdict of $18 million dollars for the estate of a man killed in a mud cave-in at a construction site, the men involved on the defense side who caused the death began to die. There were four deaths all told and Margaret Espinoza and her team failed even to make an arrest. They all were low lifes so their value to society was only enhanced by their premature departure from it but it was still frustrating on the one hand and refreshingly invigorating on the other. It wasn't just a cold case, it was a freezer case but it had been the springboard for getting her back on her horse.

She got to her condominium town house, a small two bedroom, two bath place near the Heights east of downtown, got a bath, and went through a fairly meager wardrobe to find anything but work clothes to wear. She did find a "little something" that she hadn't worn in years but that still fit with all of the exercising she did. She checked herself out in the mirror and was surprised at who looked back. Kind of sexy, a little make up to highlight the eyes, and a little cleavage to show off. Her father used to say 'if you got it, flaunt it' and tonight she thought 'what the hell.'

She heard the doorbell ring and she walked down the stairs of her townhouse. She opened the door and was pleasantly surprised by the look J.D. Rawlings gave her as he surveyed the Chief of Homicide who tonight was anything but.

"You're beautiful, Margaret."

She smiled. "First time you noticed, J.D.?"

"I hope like hell it won't be the last. May I ask you something, though?"

"Sure."

"Where do you put the gun?"

She laughed. "Can't tell you or I'd have to kill you."

It was his turn to laugh. "Fair enough. I'm starved. Seasons all right?"

"Perfect." It was one of her favorite places in Old Town and a fixture in Albuquerque for years.

In truth, she carried a small purse that had just three things in it – a key to the front door, lipstick, and her .22 caliber ankle gun.

Dinner was more fun than she had had in a long time. There was a commonality to what they did that made conversation easy and, while they promised they wouldn't talk about specific cases, they knew so many of the same people that it was like they had known each far longer than they had. The wine may have helped as well especially with a second glass provided by Will Bennett and Alex Kennedy who were having a date night at a table across the restaurant and who had seen Margaret and J.D. walk in. It was the perfect storm for a first date.

"Geez, Alex, she looks beautiful, doesn't she? Wonder where she puts the gun?"

"Shut up, Will, and get your tongue back in your mouth before somebody steps on it. And yes, she looks great."

J.D. was divorced and had been single for a number of years. They shared a common tragedy as well as their common careers in law enforcement. J.D. had lost his only child, a daughter, to a drunk driver four years ago. Margaret had remembered that half way through dinner and, although it didn't come up, it was an unspoken bond between the two of them.

Her took her home and she thought about inviting him in but it was a week night and both had much to do on the morrow. She kissed him lightly on the lips and thanked him for what truly had been a wonderful time.

"May I see you again, Margaret?"

"I sure hope so. Night."

"Night."

She closed the door and thought to herself 'wowser!'

Chapter Twelve

A Whim

The next morning, Margaret was in one of the headquarters conference rooms meeting with the team working on what the media was calling the "Tenderloin Murders." The 'john' who by all accounts was the shooter had disappeared off the face of the earth. They had no idea whether he was even still in the area and had only the murkiest of descriptions to go on simply because he'd shot everybody who could identify him. It was beginning to look like a long shot cold case and it had only been two days.

When she walked out of the meeting and was on her way to her office, her mind returned to the Jiménez deaths of father, mother and son. Not sure why at that moment but Margaret Espinosa had learned over the years to let her instincts lead her and this morning it led her to want to go out to the Desert Drive house one more time.

She took her time and her thoughts wandered back to the night before with J.D. Rawlings. She was having warm and fuzzy thoughts that hadn't been a part of her forever and she liked the feeling.

When she got to 1305, she pulled in the driveway. As she approached, she could have sworn she saw a shadow of something behind the house. She couldn't tell what it was or even if maybe she had imagined it. She parked and got out of her unmarked and walked the perimeter. The place looked to be in the same state of disrepair as the last time she had been there and she wondered what would happen to it now that the owners were dead. She vaguely remembered that Esther had a couple of sisters and she assumed they would inherit the property and hopefully get it cleaned up and sold.

In the back there was still police tape around the meth lab although it was sagging from age and lack of interest or follow up by the cops. 'What was there to follow up on anyways?' she thought to herself. She next went to the garden shed and for the first time noticed there was a dead bolt on the outside of the door. That wouldn't be unusual she thought but there wasn't a padlock on it so she opened the door.

The mattress and clothes weren't there anymore having been taken by the CIU team but everything else like the tools were still in place. She turned to leave and then noticed that there was also a dead bolt on the inside of the door as well. And that made no sense whatsoever.

'Why the hell would you have dead bolts on both sides of a garden shed door?' And then it occurred to her that it might be to keep somebody from getting in if somebody else were inside. One more question to which there was no answer.

When Margaret got back and was walking to her office, there were a few whistles from the men at their desks which was at best unprofessional and at worst showed a complete lack of respect for her and her position. That sure as hell was going to stop as of the next staff meeting. And then she got to her office door and she saw a dozen long stemmed yellow roses in a vase on her desk. She immediately blushed, got in her office as quickly as she could, and shut the door. The card was from J.D.: "Thanks for a wondrous night. Let's do it again soon. J.D." Wowser.

She called to thank him and then things got seriously weird.

"Glad you called. You remember the PD, Ginny Beckwith, who represents Mendez? She just called with a very strange tale. She and the two other PDs representing Jiménez and Torres got together for coffee this morning and her two colleagues told her that both of their clients had told their lawyers that Mendez was passed out on the couch, Pablo had gone to the bathroom, and the two of them were watching pro wrestling on a cable channel. They remembered the match and the names of the wrestlers, too. Two different identical stories to two different lawyers."

She knew a punch line was coming. "OKaaay."

Rawlings paused for the dramatic effect. "The power had been shut off six days before Pablo was killed. There's no way they could have been watching TV, cable or otherwise."

Silence for maybe thirty seconds as Margaret Espinoza tried to get her arms around one more mystery.

"Margaret?"

"I'm here, J.D. I just am having a hard time sorting it out in my head."

"Me too. I figure Beckwith and the others are probably violating attorney-client privileges out the wazoo even if they're all in the same office and I think Beckwith is telling us to give Mendez a little more help with his plea but this truly is beyond the pale. Let's the two of us think on it and circle back, OK?"

"Yep."

"One more thing. Dinner Saturday?" Her heart skipped a beat. She thought about saying something like she'd have to check her calendar but why the hell do that.

"I'd love to, J.D. What time?"

They made the date and Margaret decided it was time to do a little shopping for herself.

Chapter Thirteen

Anthony

Monday morning found Will at his desk with the wonderful feeling that there was nothing on the calendar and a full day to catch up on whatever needed catching up on. He was for the most part a contented man – loved his wife although she could be crazy making, had a wonderful job most of the time, and worked with remarkable people. So with a full day ahead of him, life was pretty damn good.

Then the receptionist called him.

"There's a young man in the lobby who says he needs to see you."

Will checked his calendar again to confirm there was nothing on the book.

"What's his name?"

Pause. "Anthony."

He didn't think he knew anybody named Anthony.

"Anthony who?"

Another pause and this time when Bethany came back, Will sensed a nervousness in her voice. "Anthony Jiménez."

That stopped him. Jiménez was a very common Hispanic name for sure but this was too much of a coincidence.

"I'll be right out. Would you sign me up for one of the conference rooms off the lobby?"

"Yes, Mr. Bennett." Again the nervousness.

Will walked to the lobby not knowing what to expect which was a good thing looking back, because what he found was like nothing he'd ever encountered before. He understood Bethany's nervousness.

Anthony Jiménez was maybe 5'2", if that, judging by how little space he took up in the waiting room chair. He couldn't have weighed more than a hundred pounds coming out of the shower although judging by the man's appearance, a shower had not been on his list of things to do for quite some time. His face was almost elf-like in appearance, thin to the point of emaciation, eyes too close together, scraggly facial hair that matched the brown hair on his head which needed a good haircut and a shampoo, ears that seemed to stick out of his narrow head and ended in points. Altogether a picture of somebody who looked like he'd been put together by an evil genius in a failed experiment. His clothes consisted of a T-shirt that was way past its best days, jeans that were worse than that, and flip flops that were way too big for two very small feet. Maybe mid-twenties in age although that was just a guess.

"Mr. Jiménez?" Will stuck out his hand. Anthony Jiménez got out of the chair and reached for Will's hand with a tiny, almost childlike hand that had the longest fingernails Will had ever seen without help from a beauty salon. They shook hands and Will was careful not to squeeze too hard. He ushered the young man into the conference room off the lobby and said to Bethany, "Would you see if either Liz, Jackie or Rosalind could join us?"

"May I get you some coffee or water, Mr. Jiménez?"

Elf man shook his head.

"Sit down," gesturing to a chair. Will sat as well and just then Jackie walked in. If she was surprised by the appearance of their guest, her face showed none of it. She introduced herself, poured a cup of coffee, and sat down.

"What can we do for you?"

The man began to speak in a voice that matched his physical appearance. Later Jackie and Will would compare notes and come to the same conclusion. It was like he had inhaled helium only it never wore off and got back to normal. This was his voice.

For the next two hours, Anthony Jiménez told a story of horror and sadness that sent chills down Will's spine. If it were true and they both were convinced it was, it was one of the most depraved, awful tales of human tragedy either had ever heard. It was told in that thin voice without any affect whatsoever as though all emotion had been wrung out of the young man because of what had been done to him.

He was the youngest son of Roberto and Esther Jiménez. Because he was "different" his parents kept him at home on Desert Drive more often than not locked in his bedroom. They would bring him food, let him use the bathroom, and otherwise kept him behind locked doors. Beginning around the age of five – although he couldn't be sure – he would get visits from his father or his two older brothers, Pablo and José. They would do things to him that he didn't understand and make him do things to them. A lot of it hurt. Anthony didn't know what was happening and didn't know right from wrong. It was simply his life. The abuse went on regularly for years as he grew into adolescence. He never left the house except for some times, they let him go outside in the yard. He never went to school and never met another human being other than his father, mother and two brothers. As he got older, he began to sense that what was being done to him was wrong although he told Jackie and Will that he had no idea where that concept came from.

Then about four years ago when he was in his bedroom he heard a terrible fight between his parents and his brothers. There were loud voices, screaming, and the sound of things banging downstairs. Finally, the noise stopped and it was silent for a time. Then the door to his bed room opened and his mother came in. She had a wash cloth pressed to the side of her face and her lower lip was bleeding. She told him to gather his things and they went downstairs, out the door, and into the family car. It was the first time in his life that he had ever been in a car. His dad was behind the wheel. His brothers were nowhere to be found. That night, they stayed in a motel and the next day moved into an apartment. He had his own bedroom like at the house and, like at the house, he was locked in it most of the time. It was better here because his brothers weren't around but his father would still come in and do things to him and he remembered his mother also being in the bedroom watching.

Jiménez was not certain how long he had been at the apartment. He could tell seasons were passing from his bedroom window and he knew when it was day or night but he had no other way to tell time or know what year it was or what day it was. One day his mother came into his bedroom, packed up what meager belongings there were, and took him out to the car. His father drove to the house on Desert Drive and when they got there, his mother threw his clothes out of the car and told Anthony to get out. He did and his parents drove off.

The front door opened and Pablo came out, picked up the clothes, grabbed Anthony by the arm and took him to the garden shed. There was a mattress on the floor and Pablo threw him on it, took his clothes off, and anally raped him. When he was done,

Pablo got up and left Anthony crying on the mattress. He shut the door and Anthony could hear the door lock. From then on, almost daily, Pablo would come to the garden shed, let Anthony go to the outhouse, and then take him back in the shed and do it all again. Sometimes he would make Anthony use his mouth and sometimes he would anally rape him. Sometimes both.

At some point and Anthony really didn't know when, José joined in the abuse as well. They fed him scraps and let him have a jar of peanut butter and some bread and a gallon jug of water and that was it. One or two trips to the outhouse a day and when Anthony sometimes couldn't hold it and had to go in the garden shed, the brothers would beat him.

Then one day it all stopped. Pablo had forgotten to lock the door one morning and left it ajar enough so Anthony could see out. He sat in the shed for hours looking out and trying to decide what to do. He thought about running into the woods but had no idea where to go or even where he was. He couldn't go to the house because they'd just put him back in the shed and beat him. He thought about going out to the road and having somebody pick him up but he knew enough that nobody would want to give somebody like him a ride. Plus he had to get past the house to get to the road and if they saw him, they'd get him that way as well. He sat paralyzed for what seemed like a very long time although Anthony really had no sense of how to tell time.

Then two very strange things happened. A cell phone went off in the shed and Anthony realized that the phone had dropped out of Pablo's pants. He didn't answer it. And then he heard a very loud bang coming from the house. He didn't know what it was but it scared him. Somewhere in the recesses of his mind, he had come to learn about 911 and he picked up the phone and called it and left a message. He waited.

A few minutes later he saw a police car drive down the driveway and pull up to the house. He opened the door to the shed and ran into the woods behind the out buildings. From that vantage point he watched for a long time as lots of police officers arrived. He saw them search his shed and the other building and pretty soon he saw his brother, José, and two other men being led out to some of the police cars and driven off. Then something was rolled out on a bed with wheels and put in a long black car. All of a sudden, everything was quiet. There was lots of yellow tape around the house but Anthony ducked under it, found the key in the flower pot where his mother had put it years ago, and went inside. He had lived there ever since. The only time he was ever bothered was when a car drove up and a woman got out. He recognized her from the day all the police were there and ran out the back door into the woods and hid until she left.

There were lots more questions than answers.

"How did you know to come here, Anthony?"

"One day at the apartment after Daddy came in and touched me, he got up to put his pants on and some change and a card fell out. I picked it up and kept it. I remembered all the letters and found an old phone book at the house. I matched the name on the card to here."

"How did you get here?"

"Walk."

Jackie. "Are you hungry, Anthony?"

"Yes, ma'am. Real hungry."

"What have you been living on these last weeks?"

"Stuff that was left over when they all left. Caught a rabbit and made a fire. Not much."

"You wait here for a minute. Mr. Bennett and I need to talk, OK?"

"OK."

Will and Jackie went into Will's office.

"I feel like I'm gonna throw up, Jackie. This is sick beyond anything I've ever heard."

"Yep, it is. I think the first thing is we get some food for the kid. Second thing is we have to get the power back on. Got a friend at the power company and let me give him a call right now. The we can take him home and then figure out what we're going to do. You OK with that?"

Will got his friend on the phone, called in a couple – well, more than a couple – favors plus Will's credit card for the arrears and his friend promised the power back on within the hour.

They stopped at a healthy fast food restaurant and got Anthony a sandwich. He began to devour it and they had him slow down a notch or two to make sure he just didn't throw it back up. Then they got a couple more sandwiches to go and made a stop at a grocery store to get some milk and some easy to fix food. Next stop was a department store to get him some underwear and new pants and shirts. The last stop was 1305 Desert Drive.

Jackie and Will followed him into the house with the bags and were both surprised. The place spotless.

"You do this, Anthony?" Jackie's are outstretched to indicate the room.

He nodded. *"I wanted to be clean."*

"Do you take showers or a bath?"

"No power. Don't know how."

"Can we show you while we're here?" Will checked and the power was on, checked the hot water heater and it was on. He reminded himself to send his friend a thank you card.

Anthony pointed to Jackie. *"You."*

The two went off together and came back in about 20 minutes. Anthony Jiménez looked like a new man, clean for the first time in forever, and in new clothes. Will wondered if this was the first time the young man had ever had anything new to wear in his life. Probably. But Will was sure of one thing. This was the first time in Anthony's life that human kindness had touched him.

They made sure that Anthony would be all right if they left him although that was a little silly given he'd been living in this place for weeks all by himself. They told him they'd be back in a day or two. He went up to Jackie and hugged her goodbye. She turned to leave and Will saw tears in her eyes.

'Now that truly is something you don't see every day.'

Chapter Fourteen

Dilemma

On the way back to the office, they began to unpeel this onion called Anthony Jiménez. Will's first thought was to get Anthony into some sort of state supervised adult foster care until Jackie said quietly, "You think he killed Pablo?"

They pondered that for a while. Anthony was no dummy and although he couldn't read or write, it wasn't for lack of intelligence. Could he have spun his tale to Jackie and Will and simply left out the part about killing his brother? Hard to say but not outside the realm of possibility. The nature of the killing and the rage it reflected could certainly have come at the hands of a young man who had been sexually brutalized his entire life. Talk about justifiable homicide. But where's the gun, where did the bottle of perfume come from? If the state became involved in his care, he clearly would come under the scrutiny of the Albuquerque Police Department and in particular one Margaret Espinoza, Chief of the Homicide Division. That wouldn't be good and neither Will nor Jackie wanted to be the one to rat him out.

On the other hand, he had no skills in life and could not ultimately live on his own. That was clear. One puzzle was what was wrong with him physically and mentally. He clearly was developmentally disabled and perhaps belonged somewhere on the autism spectrum. But even with his illiteracy, he could communicate clearly with speech. What the years of abuse did to his brain was anybody's guess but, from a lay person's perspective, it was likely never to be fixed.

"You know, Will. We say he can't live on his own but look at what he's been doing. He's survived everything that's been done to him."

"Sure, but he'd starve to death. If we hadn't bought him food, where's the next meal coming from? And what's he going to use for money – if he even knows what money is? And personal hygiene? That's probably the first time he's washed in years – if ever. We gotta do something."

Jackie wondered about Anthony living with Josephine and her but that would be nigh on to impossible. Both of them were far too busy to give the young man the kind of attention he would need. At the same time, Will was having the same thought about him moving in with Alex and him but he dismissed it for an entirely different reason – selfishness. He and Alex had gotten to the point in life where they wanted nothing more than to be just the two of them. And the cats. Adding Anthony to the mix would bring layers of complications that he didn't want. At least he was being honest.

So the answer would have to be to find a private foster care situation that wasn't licensed by the State of New Mexico and would fly under the radar. Neither of them had a clue where the hell they would find that. Plus where would the money come from to first of all pay for the foster care and second, pay for the therapy and education to give Anthony any chance at all in life?

That night, he got a drink for Alex and himself and they sat out on the patio while Will filled her in on the day's activities. She listened to it all in silence and Will could almost see the wheels turning as she mulled over what he was telling her. He just knew she'd have some ideas on a course of action.

"Jesus, Will. I have no idea whatsoever about what to do."

OK, well that didn't go quite like he'd hoped. She had liked the idea of a private foster care setting but how to pay for it was the problem. She estimated, adding in the therapy and special tutors, that the foster care package would come to something more than a couple of hundred grand a year. They wondered about private foundation money or some sort of private grant but neither had a clue how to go about that. Will set up the Felipe Ruiz Foundation with the proceeds from the trial he had after the construction cave in but that money was committed to helping disadvantaged youth in Albuquerque and its assets couldn't take this kind of a hit and still do what it was doing.

For the next two weeks, Will and Jackie settled into a routine. Usually Jackie or sometimes Jackie and Will together would go out to the house on Desert Drive and check on Anthony Jiménez. Will never went alone given Anthony's fear of anything male. One day, Jackie took her spouse, Josephine Lucas, out to see him. Josephine was an anesthesiologist by trade but knew enough from medical school days to do a physical exam. Anthony turned out to be remarkably healthy. A couple of days later, they got him to the University of New Mexico free dental clinic registering him under a fake name. That visit was to be one of several for the young man as dental hygiene had not been a high priority for any of the Jiménez clan that had brutalized him. Cavities were filled and dental hygiene improved dramatically.

Jackie would make several meals at once and leave them in the refrigerator or freezer with instructions on how to heat them and eat them. Even in two weeks' time, Anthony's color was better and he was putting on some weight.

Chapter Fifteen

Rita

Will was running out of options. They couldn't just leave Anthony Jiménez at Desert Drive for the rest of his life running food and clothing out to him on a daily basis. So he decided to bite the bullet and call Rita Alverson, a longtime friend and arguably the best criminal defense lawyer in the state if not the entire Southwest. They met for lunch with Will buying because whatever happened and whether Rita got involved or not, they were both going to be working for free.

Rita was one of the smartest and toughest lawyers Will had ever met. Plus she was a knockout beautiful red head who, like Alex, seemed to get more beautiful with age. There had been a time when Will and Rita had first gotten to know each other that there had been a flicker of something – more likely than not, pure lust – but they had had the good sense not to act on it leaving both their friendship, Rita's friendship with Alex, and Will and Alex's relationship all intact. While Will preferred a quick green chile cheeseburger at his desk for lunch, he splurged and they met at Yanni's in Nob Hill. Small talk over, Will got down to what was up.

Alverson listened carefully, asked some questions along the way, and when he was done, simply said: "You've got to turn him in, Will. You can't be in a position of harboring at worst a fugitive and, at best, a 'person of interest.' You could lose your bar ticket for something like this."

He was pretty sure that was going to be the advice he was going to get but he pushed back.

"Rita, this man child has been abused all of his life. Let's say he killed Pablo. So what? Son of a bitch deserved it."

"Doesn't matter, my friend, and you know in your heart of hearts, it doesn't matter. What happened to him all gets taken into account once he's in the legal system but you can't be playing God all by yourself just 'cause of it."

"What about a lie detector?"

"What if he flunks it? Plus the reliability is going to be very iffy given his disabilities."

"Will you represent him?"

"Gratis, I assume."

"That's why we're at Yanni's, Rita."

She laughed, "I figured it was something like that. OK, so I want to meet this young man as soon as possible. Will he first of all understand what we're asking of him and, second, give himself up willingly?"

"Best chance is to take Jackie LaPointe with us. She seems to be the only one he trusts."

"This afternoon?"

"Yep."

Will called Jackie from the restaurant and her schedule was clear. They dropped Rita's car off at her office, picked up Jackie, and drove to Desert Drive.

When Anthony saw the car come into the driveway, he ran out of the house, hugged Jackie as soon as she got out of the car, and completely ignored Will and Rita. Over the next half hour with Jackie doing most of the talking and with Rita adding what she could, it came down to Anthony having to make a decision.

"What should I do, Jackie?"

"The only thing you can do, Anthony. Trust Rita and Will and me."

"OK." Not much more than a whisper.

They left him at the house and told him they would probably be back the next day. He hugged Jackie good bye and again she got in the car with tears in her eyes.

Jackie LaPointe was one of the toughest people Will had ever met, having endured an awful lot in her young life before Will and Alex had met her. And that clearly was the human connection between Jackie and Anthony. She got it.

On the way back to downtown, Rita had a thought.

"If he turns himself in and if he didn't do it or if he didn't have the mental capacity to do it, why don't you sue somebody?"

"Like who?"

"Open estates for the mom and dad and sue them. They've at least got the house and maybe some other stuff. José as well. Maybe even an estate for Pablo. Least you can do and this way, I can think that maybe I'll get paid some day." She smiled and Will knew she would go to the mat for Anthony whether she got paid or not.

But the thought lingered and, after they dropped Rita off, Jackie and Will noodled it.

"Once it all hits the fan, won't matter a bit, Will. Hell, even if he's guilty, a jury might well give him some money for what he's been through."

"Any way to check on what Esther and Roberto had in savings or investments on the QT?"

"Call Robert. He's always got something up his sleeve."

Robert Davison a life time ago had been with the Alexandria Police Department trying to find Will Bennett's best friend who he was absolutely convinced had killed his wife. Over the course of the investigation that almost got Will killed, Robert and Will had become good friends. Robert had gone on to marry Alicia Dawe, Chief of Homicide for the Alexandria Police Department, and they had had two children together bringing a blended family of his kids, Alicia's sister's kids when her sister had been killed in a drive by, and now their own additions. Alicia was still with the police but Robert had gone out on his own as a private detective.

"Perfect."

Chapter Sixteen

Jackpot

Will got hold of Robert on his cell phone at his house in Northern Virginia. Surprisingly, Robert was taking a rare day off and staying home with the kids while Alicia stamped out injustice with the Alexandria Police Department. The two men, so different in so many ways, had become close friends even with the distance and usually talked two or three times a month. This wasn't the first time Will had called on his friend for help and it wasn't very long before Robert cut to the chase.

"So whadda you need, Bud?" Always to the point.

"Well, to make a short story long…" Will gave Robert the details of what they knew so far, told him about the man child, and then asked whether Robert had any ability to access data banks to determine the assets of Esther and Robert Jiménez late of Albuquerque, New Mexico.

"Soc numbers?"

"Nope. All I got is a house they own in Albuquerque and their apartment address here."

"Geez, don't ask for much, do you? OK, give me what you got and let me see what I can do."

"Thanks, Robert. You guys got time to hook up in Michigan next summer?"

"You kiddin'? That place is magical for us, you know that, Will." He did indeed know it was magical having been awakened in the middle of the night with noises in the downstairs bedroom that had led to the conception of their youngest daughter, Katherine.

"Still think you shoulda called her Willamena or at least Alexandra."

"Sorry. We'll make it up to you somehow. Lemme get on this and I'll call you back if I can find anything out." They rang off.

Will spent the rest of the afternoon catching up on his files and got home just ahead of Alex. They ordered take out from Duran's across the way and Will walked over to pick it up. When he got back, Alex was on his cell phone and it didn't take long to figure out it was Robert. Will had never understood the relationship between his spouse and Robert and that was probably a good thing because there had been a time when Alexandra Kennedy had an eye on her husband's friend. Nothing ever came of it but the two of them had a closeness that, if he thought about it enough, Will would react to with jealousy. At any rate, the small talk ran out and Alex handed the phone over to Will.

"Hey."

"Hey yourself, my friend. I think you may have hit the jackpot on this one."

"Why so?"

"You forgot to tell me the house on Desert Drive also included 200 acres behind it that butts up to one of the main irrigation ditches that feeds the farms a little farther south of Desert Drive. As I understand it, that makes this place a gold mine. SEV is $400k so roughly double it and you're looking at a property that may be worth something in excess of $800k. One other thing that you may find interesting. Long time ago, Esther and Roberto took out life insurance policies of $500,000 with each other as the primary beneficiaries. If they were both dead…which they are…secondary beneficiaries are Pablo and José. No mention of Anthony. Both policies are up to date so total assuming you could get a judgment against José, you're looking at around $1.8 million. And the two year exemption for suicide is way past so if you can get Anthony to be the beneficiary in place of his brothers, cool. And no will on file for either of them. Even for a shooter like you, Will, that ain't chump change."

Will was stunned. But it didn't take long for the wheels to start turning.

"Wow."

"One way to put it. Keep me posted. Alicia's due home any minute and I gotta get the burgers going."

"Robert, I don't know how…"

"Save it. You'll make it up to me next summer. Oh, one more thing. Don't ever ask me how I got this information. I'd have to kill you. Love to you both." He hung up.

Will looked at Alex. "Bingo."

<h1 style="text-align:center">Chapter Seventeen</h1>

<h2 style="text-align:center">The Wheels of Justice Begin to Turn</h2>

The next day, Will met with Rosalind, Jackie and Liz. The first order of business was to petition the Bernalillo County Probate Court to open estates for Roberto, Esther and Pablo Jiménez. An initial check with the court showed that nothing had been filed so far even though Esther apparently had those two sisters who lived in Mexico. Second order of business was to file a petition with the same probate court to have Jackie LaPointe appointed Guardian for Anthony Jiménez which, if granted, would give Jackie the authority to act in his best interests. Third order of business was to prepare a complaint in which Jackie LaPointe as Guardian for Anthony Jiménez sued the Estates of Roberto Jiménez, Esther Jiménez, Pablo Jiménez and José Jiménez individually for the years of sexual assault on Anthony. Rosalind was given the responsibility of preparing the necessary documents for filing with the Court.

The final order of business that morning was for Will to call Margaret Espinoza and set up a meeting with her, Rita Alverson, Jackie LaPointe, Will and Anthony. He got her voice mail on her cell and asked that she call him back as soon as she could. What he couldn't have known was that Margaret had taken a rare day off to go shopping for herself. This was one day she wanted for herself. So it wasn't until late in the afternoon that she returned the call having gotten the packages home and unpacked.

"Will?"

"You sitting down, Margaret?"

"I can be. What's up?"

"There's a third Jiménez brother."

Silence for several seconds as Margaret digested it.

"Tell me about it."

Will filled her in on the details, how Anthony Jiménez had found his way to his office via the business card that had been in Pablo's pocket, what he had told Will and Jackie about his life, Will's amateur diagnosis of Anthony, and where he was living. Margaret flashed on the movement she had seen in the back of the Desert Drive address when she had pulled up.

"I've asked Rita Alverson to represent him because I know you will have lots of questions for him."

"I understand, Will. When can I meet him?"

"I'll check with Rita's schedule but how 'bout tomorrow morning at Rita's office. Say 10?"

"Yep."

Rita was fine with 10:00 and Will and Jackie went out to the house on Desert Drive to make certain Anthony would be available. He was scared but Jackie comforted him and said she'd be back the next morning to make certain he got a shower and was dressed in his new clothes.

"I love you, Jackie."

"I love you too, Anthony. See you tomorrow and make sure you get good sleep tonight, OK?"

"OK."

On the way back into town, Will called Margaret and confirmed the meeting.

Chapter Eighteen

Friday the Thirteenth

Will Bennett by nature was not a particularly superstitious person. Sure, there were a few eccentricities. When he was in trial he always wore the same pair of socks and washed them if the case was going into a second week. He always wore the same purple tie on the first day of trial figuring everybody else would be wearing a red one (and invariably he was right). And he always wore the same pair of underwear (clean) and the same suit for closing arguments. Other than that, he felt himself to be completely free of the many neuroses that seemed to bother his brother and sister trial lawyers.

Nevertheless, when he realized that it was Friday the 13th of November when Margaret Espinoza was going to meet Anthony Jiménez for the first time, he got a very bad feeling. He dressed and as usual got to the office early, made the first pot of coffee, and then had some time to schmooze with Morton Blackwell, one of the founding members of the firm, and a man who Will considered one of his closest friends. Given the whirl of events over the past several days, Will hadn't had the chance to catch Morton up with the Jiménez case and so filled him in.

About 9:00, Jackie LaPointe arrived with Anthony Jiménez in tow. He was clean-shaven and dressed in his new duds.

"Anthony, you look great, man. You really do. You OK?"

"I guess so, Will. As long as you and Jackie are with me."

"It's all going to be fine and Rita will be a big help. No worries."

The three of them walked the block and a half to Rita's office. Rita Alverson was the black sheep of her firm, a well-heeled, silk stocking group of Republicans in a blue state who represented most of the major businesses and rich people in New Mexico. The problem for the firm was that on an almost daily basis, its rich clients were getting themselves into major difficulties, many of them criminal, and so Rita, for a ridiculous amount of money, was there to do her best to bail them out of whatever they had gotten themselves into. And she was good, no doubt about it. But what Rita had that her partners were devoid of, at least in Will's estimation, was heart. And so when Anthony Jiménez fell into his lap and he knew the police would be looking at him as what they euphemistically call a "person of interest," Rita was who he called.

Rita spent the next half hour explaining to Anthony what was going to happen when they met Detective Espinoza. He never let go of Jackie's hand.

"Tell the truth, Anthony. That's the main thing. OK?" She usually told her clients in a situation like this to 'tell the truth briefly' but that would have been lost on her young client.

At promptly 10:00, the receptionist announced Detective Espinoza's arrival.

If Margaret Espinoza was surprised at Anthony Jiménez's appearance, her face showed no reaction whatsoever. She was polite and professional, explained that she had some questions to ask, and promised that if his lawyer didn't want him to answer a question, she would respect that.

This was not the first rodeo for Rita Alverson and Margaret Espinoza. When Rita was with the Public Defender, they had crossed paths on any number of occasions and had begrudgingly developed a respect for each other. Now that Rita was dealing with a different kind of criminal that usually, but not always, didn't include homicide, they didn't see or confront each other as much as they used to. But the respect had survived. And when Margaret's son was killed, Rita Alverson was one of the people who reached out to her in her grief. Margaret would not forget that.

The interview itself lasted for 90 minutes, Margaret asked the questions and Anthony in his sing song helium voice answered them. Rita didn't interrupt once and Anthony answered without any emotion whatsoever.

When she was done, she asked to meet with Rita, Will and Jackie but Anthony wouldn't let go of Jackie so she stayed with Anthony.

"Thank you for your time, Mr. Jiménez. I'm sorry this has all happened to you."

"Thank you. It was nice meeting you." He shook hands with his left hand because his right was in Jackie's hand.

Will, Rita and Margaret went to Rita's office. Will always thought Rita's office looked a bit like a bordello with lots of dark red drapes, dark red fabric on the chairs, and low almost romantic lighting. But he wasn't going to argue with her success or her reputation and, if it suited her, so be it. Plus he was pretty sure at the end of the day it was a jab at her blue blood partners with their fancy cars and fancy clients and fancy country clubs. Nothing like having some red drapes and low lighting in a Republican stronghold.

Margaret let her hair down just a bit when it was just the three of them.

"Jesus F Christ, how do people do this to children? Jesus F Christ."

"Been a long time since I was with the PD, but this is one of the worst I've ever seen. Perfect storm of a young person with significant problems through no fault of his own who then becomes a victim of some truly awful people...his parents and his brothers."

Will. "You like him for Pablo's murder, Margaret?"

She seemed startled by the question as though it was the first time she had considered it. She paused for a moment.

"I guess it's possible but hard to imagine a young person with his kind of disabilities could have put it together to do it." And to herself, she thought even if he did do it, talk about justifiable homicide. Jesus F Christ. To the others, "I want to think about that for a while, just to walk it through."

She stood to leave. "What's going to happen to him?"

"We're not sure at this point. I think we're going to have to get him into some sort of adult foster care, I guess, but I'm not sure the State of New Mexico is prepared for the likes of Anthony Jiménez. In the meantime, we're going to leave him at the Desert Drive house. It's the only place he's really known and, frankly, the place is cleaner than it's been in years. Jackie sees him once or twice a day and keeps him clean and fed. We're filing suit against his parents' estates, his brother's estate, and his brother. We think there may be some money there so maybe we can make his life a little better."

"Do you think he killed Pablo, Will?" Will glanced at Rita who looked like she was about to stroke.

"I don't, Margaret, I really don't. Even after everything that's happened to him, he is a sweet young man."

"I'll be in touch. Thanks, Rita. As always, good to see you."

"You too, Margaret, take care."

After she left, Rita looked at Will. "Nice catch on that last question but here's some very important advice. Don't ever in your wildest dreams think about doing criminal defense work. Promise?"

"Promise, Rita. Thanks."

He gathered up Jackie and Anthony and got Anthony home. They weren't home free by any stretch but a good way down the road.

Chapter Nineteen

Saturday the Fourteenth

Saturday in Albuquerque dawned with a beautiful cobalt blue sky and a promise of warmth once the chill wore off. New Mexico was arguably the poorest state in the Union by any economic or educational standards but it had two things that were immeasurably incredible. The first was its art and the legacy the likes of Georgia O'Keefe and others had left it. And the second was the climate which even a Michigander like Will Bennett had to agree was the best he'd ever lived in. Almost always sun, seasons nowhere near like Michigan but enough to know the year was passing. Snow in the northern part of New Mexico in the winter time and Will still spent a few days on the blue runs feeling the freedom of the cold air on his face and the rhythm of the skis on his feet over groomed hills. Like riding a bicycle although, for both skiing and biking, the legs didn't last as long as they used to.

And so it was that day for Margaret Espinoza as she ran errands, stopped at work long enough to catch up on a backlog of paper, and then spent the rest of the day getting nervous about her date. She pondered Anthony Jiménez to keep her mind off the coming night. She honestly didn't see him for Pablo's killing but even if he did it, she couldn't imagine he'd ever be found competent to stand trial. On the other hand, there really wasn't a long list of suspects beyond the miscreants they had found at the house. That afternoon she found the one store in Albuquerque that sold Fracas perfume, a fragrance she had loved for years but never had a reason to buy or use.

7:00 arrived, the doorbell rang, and her heart skipped. She took one more look at herself in the mirror, liked what she saw, and opened the door.

J.D. Rawling's reaction was exactly what she had hoped for.

"Wow, Margaret." In almost a whisper.

"You're not so bad yourself, J.D." He was dressed in a frilled white shirt, handsome turquoise bolo, pressed jeans and hand-crafted cowboy boots.

"I'm thinking we're way overdressed but I made reservations at the Monte Carlo. Is that OK?"

Secretly, she'd been hoping for something a little fancier than that but the fact was that she loved the Monte Carlo, an institution in Albuquerque since 1970, and, truth be known, was far more her style than anything fancier. It was a concrete building that had a package liquor store in front, great steaks, even better prime rib if you got there early enough, and a wine list that was decent – and affordable. And a good pour on the liquor. What more could you ask?

"Perfect."

They arrived and Margaret realized she could have used at least a shawl to cover bare shoulders. Late fall in New Mexico, the chill came early. But they got in without goose bumps and J.D. had reserved a corner booth for them. They both commented that the Monte Carlo had upgraded its red faux leather to replace the cracked stuff that had been there forever and both of them felt better about being the best dressed couple in the place.

The night was like the Monte Carlo…comfortable. They talked some about work but didn't dwell. Margaret made it a point not to talk about Anthony Jiménez. She was still trying to figure out how it all fit, if it fit at all, and didn't want to bring a current case they were both working on into the mix. So they talked about their pasts some, talked about where they were in their careers, and talked about what the future might look like. Along the way, they realized they were more alike than different, more in sync than they might have thought, and more attuned to each other than they might have suspected given the very different paths their lives had travelled. What she really liked was that they listened to each other and responded and they were both were genuinely interested in knowing about the other. What a concept.

So maybe it was the wine and maybe it was wants and needs and maybe it was magic. She asked him to spend the night and he said that he would like to but only because it would be fun to have coffee with her in the morning.

"Well, it's a start. Or maybe a finish. Let's find out."

It had been a long time for both of them and it was awkward and a little clumsy and kind of funny and then kind of wonderful. Mostly it was very clean and very good. Sunday morning came and they woke up for the first time to get to the bathroom, got back to bed, drifted, made love, drifted and finally about 11:00 decided it was time to get up for good. She had a sweatshirt that didn't look too bad on him, dressed herself in sweats, and they went to breakfast at the Western View on Central. Over coffee and huevos rancheros, they talked out the night and what it meant.

"So. What think you?"

"J.D., what happened last night and since I met you is so wonderfully exciting and so incredibly terrifying. It's like I had shut down this whole side of me, dedicated myself to work and to Bobbie, and then after he died, to work. Then you come along and I'm like a hormonally challenged teenager. It scares the shit out of me. You?"

"It's terrifying, I get that. But…we could walk away from this or maybe, just maybe, play it out. Take it slow, get to know each other, and see if it fits."

She nodded.

"Or we could just say fuck it and get married today and live out our lives blissfully in love."

She almost choked on the eggs. "I vote for the former but I could be persuaded about the latter. Except it's Sunday."

"Wonder what Judge Kennedy is doing today?"

"The former, cowboy. Slow and easy. But let me buy you breakfast and maybe back to my place?"

Chapter Twenty

Maria

The break in the case came that Monday when a young Hispanic woman walked into the South Valley branch of the Albuquerque Police Department and announced she had information about the murder of Pablo Jiménez.

Maria Thompson was a seventeen-year-old runaway who had been living on the streets of Albuquerque since she was thirteen. She told the desk sergeant that she had been the product of alcoholic parents who were both physically and emotionally abusive and who basically drove her out of her house to save herself. She had done stints in shelters but they always asked for too much information so most of the time she spent in doorways or under bridges or in the open fields or abandoned houses that dotted the landscape especially in the Valley.

She reminded the sergeant of his granddaughter and it broke his heart to see her but the thought crossed his mind that 'there but for the Grace of God…' and he reminded himself to call his granddaughter that night when his shift ended so he could tell her how much he loved her. Maria looked older than 17 and he supposed living on the streets for four years would do that to a person, especially a young girl. She had dirty hair and could have used a long shower with a lot of soap. But for some faded acne scars, she was pretty in a tough sort of way, dressed warmly in clothes that she had either gathered from a shelter or stolen. As she told her story, her expression and her voice were completely devoid of emotion as though all feelings and emotions had been surgically removed.

Maria told him that she had early on learned that if she was going to be on the streets as a young girl, she would need protection and so, from the beginning, she would align with a male who would protect her from others. She would stay with that person for a time and then either Maria or the man would move on to something or somebody else. She didn't turn tricks as much as she paid for protection with her body. She didn't complain about it to the sergeant, it was just simply the way it was.

She told the sergeant that several weeks before she had hooked up with a man named José Jiménez who saw her standing on a street corner in downtown Albuquerque and had pulled over to talk to her. While she made it clear to him that she was not a hooker, he did tell her that she could crash at his house for a while and she took him up on it. He explained that he had just gotten out of prison and was trying to find a job but that it was difficult given his past. He was not the first ex-felon that Maria had been with in the four years on the streets and it was of little consequence to her. The house was toward the secluded south end of the Valley and a pig sty. But it was a roof over her head and for that she was grateful. He shared the house with his brother, Pablo, who seemed to be the quieter, nicer of the two brothers. That night she slept with José and for the next couple of weeks that became the pattern. Nobody left the house much except to get some food or panhandle downtown and there were plenty of drugs to keep Maria happy.

Unfortunately, one night when José was in town with some friends, Pablo and Maria were left on their own and, after a couple of hits of meth, had sex. While she was mostly indiscriminate when it came to her choice of lovers when she was living on the streets, there was no comparison between the two brothers. Pablo was a far better lover, smelled better, and even went so far as to try to satisfy Maria, a concept that was completely foreign to her. A new pattern developed in which the two men shared Maria except that José didn't know it. It all went splendidly until the night José and Maria had had sex, José passed out, and Maria went to Pablo's bedroom only to have José wake up and come upon his brother *in pari delicto* with Maria who José thought was his girlfriend. A terrible argument started and Pablo and José got into a fight that continued through the house. Maria, survivor that she was, knew that this was a story that was not going to end well for her under any circumstances and while the two men were battling it out with kitchen chairs in the dining room, she gathered what few belongings she had and lit out.   She made it to Desert Drive, hitched a ride to the bus station in Albuquerque, spent the night on the bench in the station, and the next morning was back on the streets.

It was some weeks after her escape that she happened to glance at an old *Albuquerque Journal* paper that somebody had left on a park bench and she coincidentally saw an article about the death of Pablo Jiménez at the home on Desert Drive.

And that got her to the police station.

The desk sergeant called his captain and summarized the story. Maria Thompson was taken downtown to headquarters, gave a recorded statement to a detective, and was then taken to a juvenile detention center which, in her mind, was one of the best places she had stayed since she had run away from home. Now seventeen, nobody had any authority to call her parents and, for the first time in forever, she felt safe. She knew it wouldn't last but then Maria really only lived from day to day anyways and this was good enough for this day.

Chapter Twenty One

Putting It Together

The Thompson statement crossed Margaret Espinoza's desk the next morning and as soon as she read it, she called J.D. Rawlings. They had been practically inseparable since that first weekend together and last night had been spent at her condo. Nobody was using the "love" word yet but it sure seemed to Margaret that things were moving in that direction.

J.D. had recognized the number on his phone and his first thought was maybe she was calling to set up a 'Nooner.' No such luck but he listened intently to the story and when Margaret was done asked one question. "Does Maria Thompson wear perfume?" Margaret rechecked the statement and nobody had figured to ask that question. Neither Margaret nor J.D. were surprised it hadn't come up. When did detectives taking a statement ever worry about what perfume the witness was wearing? Like never? Margaret told him she would get over to the Detention Center as soon as she could and meet Maria Thompson.

Shortly before noon, Margaret was ushered into an interview room. Maria was already there looking freshly showered and dressed in clean clothes. Having never laid eyes on her before, Margaret could only guess what she might have looked like on the streets but here in the room, her first impression was a nice enough young woman who looked older than seventeen. Like the desk sergeant who had first met her, Margaret's thoughts were that life on the streets would do that especially to a young woman. They made small talk for a while, Margaret filled in some blanks that she had from the statement taken the day before, and then Margaret popped the question: "You wear perfume, Maria?"

Taken aback, Maria thought that was about the dumbest question anybody had ever asked her. She'd been on the streets for four years living under bridges and in usually dry culverts begging for her next meal and this detective wanted to know if she wore perfume. Really?

"No, Detective, perfume is not a part of my day to day existence."

Margaret Espinoza nodded mostly to herself and stood to leave.

"How long can I stay here?" Maria asked.

Margaret turned. "How long do you want to stay here?"

The teenager thought for a minute and the idea of being back on the streets with winter coming on brought her to tears.

"Maybe a few days if that would be all right."

"Then what, Maria? Back on the streets?"

Maria shrugged. "Guess so."

"Tell you what. I'll see what I can do about you staying here for a bit." It made perfect sense because if they liked José for his brother's murder, trying to find a street perso who was the primary witness would be ridiculous especially if she didn't want to be found. "Then maybe we can get you into some sort of shelter or half way house and see if we can't make some changes for you. You OK with that?"

Tears freely now. And in a very quiet voice, "Yes, ma'am."

Margaret turned again to leave.

"Hey wait! Pablo bought me a bottle of perfume like a week before I left. Just remembered."

The detective wheeled around.

"Remember what kind, Maria?"

She thought for a minute. "Something *Mist* I think. Real pretty bottle, I do remember that. Nobody had ever done anything like that for me before."

Margaret nodded and thought to herself that the pretty bottle was in lots more different pieces than when Maria had seen it last.

It was a little after noon when she was walking out of the Center and she called J.D. on her cell. "I've got important information but I can only tell you face to face. Too classified to talk about it over the phone. My place in twenty minutes?"

"Yep." Rawlings hung up with a smile. One 'Nooner' coming up.

An hour later the couple came up for air and began to talk about the Pablo Jiménez case.

"Nothing like a good murder investigation discussion in the afterglow, right, J.D.?"

He laughed. "Keep it up and we may never get back to work."

So they had motive and opportunity. But they still had the mysteries of how the gun that killed Pablo got to the Jiménez's apartment while José was in custody.

"Enough to charge him, J.D?"

"Enough to sweat him for sure. Enough to charge? Tough case with the murder weapon showing up later although we had Esther's prints in the house. She goes there after Pablo's death, finds the gun in a place where it had been stored, takes it home, kills her husband, and then kills herself? Maybe."

Chapter Twenty Two

José

Late that afternoon, Detective Margaret Espinoza met José Jiménez and his Public Defender, Chris Patton, at the Bernalillo County Jail.

"Let me get right to it, gentlemen. We like you, José, for the murder of your brother. We've got motive because Pablo was screwing your girlfriend right under your nose, you had opportunity because you were in the same house, you smelled the perfume she wore and knew it hadn't come from you, you had the murder weapon that your family owned, and you carved 'M' on your brother's chest with the broken perfume bottle. That sure seems to me that it stands for Maria.   You wanna talk about it? Get it off your chest?" She smiled to herself. 'Get it off your chest? Geez, I just crack myself up sometimes.'

Patton asked for a few minutes to meet with his client and Margaret left the interrogation room.

A few minutes later, Patton was ushered out of the room by the guard.

"Denies everything and swears he didn't do it. Yes, he was mad about Pablo screwing his girlfriend but didn't know anything about perfume, didn't know there was a gun in the house…if there was… and wasn't in any kind of shape himself to do it even if he wanted to." He paused. "Plus you don't have the gun. So you got two out of three – motive, opportunity and no means. Takes three to tango, Detective."

She stood up and left without a word. 'Tango this, asshole.'

Chapter Twenty Three

Making the Case

The next morning, Rawlings, Espinoza, Detective Bill Anderson and Detective Howard Bunker met in Rawlings' conference room and went over what they had. Motive and opportunity, they had locked but means was a problem and the only reasonable explanation, if José killed his brother, was that Esther came to the house later when it was empty and took the gun from some hiding place known only to the family and not found by the police, took it back to the apartment, and committed the murder/suicide. There was not one piece of credible evidence to suggest that scenario except for Esther's fingerprints in the dining area of the house she had lived in for years. Another loose end floated to the service. They couldn't figure out for the life of them how José Jiménez and Juan Torres could possibly have been watching the same TV show at exactly the same moment with the power off.

"Cell phone instead of TV?" Anderson offered.

"Yeah, maybe. But they're both so sure it was the TV. Why lie about that?" Bunker.

"Too drugged up to know the difference? Shit, I have no idea."

Rawlings. "Let's do this. Bill and Howard, you guys get with Mendez and Torres and their suits, tell them we like José for Pablo's murder, and tell them we like them both for Accessory to Murder. Squeeze them and see what oozes out. Plus whoever gets Torres, push on the whole TV thing. Not sure it makes a difference but I'd sure like to know the answer. Honestly, regardless of what they say – and I'm guessing it won't be much – I'm still thinking of taking a flyer at José for his brother's murder. The perfume bottle and the 'M' tip me over the edge. Margaret, if you don't mind, would you go see Maria Thompson one more time? I'd like to know a little more about the perfume, when he gave it to her, how he gave it to her, and anything else you can think of. Plus I wonder if she ever met Torres and Mendez or if she was out of there before they got there. And here's another thing that doesn't make sense. José catches Pablo and Maria in the rack, there's a huge fight that takes place all over the house, Maria runs for her life, some days later apparently, Mendez and Torres move in, and it's only then that Pablo buys it. Seems like it would have gone down the night of the fight. Why would he wait days and then kill with the rage he does?"

There was silence for a moment and suddenly Margaret realized all three men were looking at her.

"Margaret, you OK?"

She had actually been off on a reverie thinking about the night before with J.D. and the sex and his body lying next to her and his soft breathing when he'd fallen asleep. She had gone for a long long time without a man and now was closing in on nymphomania. She hadn't heard a word that had been said after 'Shit, I have no idea.'

"Sorry." She stood up. "I'm all over it."

Bunker and Anderson left and Rawlings stopped her for a moment.

"Do you know what you're doing next?"

"Honestly, not a clue. My mind wandered."

"Care to tell me where?"

"Yeah, I think you're putting something in my drink at night so I can't keep my hands off you. Am I right?"

"Hey, if you need to believe that, then yes, of course. Wonder if there's any other reason?"

"Has to be the only explanation. So what am I doing?"

J.D. went over her visiting Maria Thompson one more time, hugged her good bye, and let her out of the conference room. He stopped for a moment before he left. It had been forever since a woman had touched him this deeply and in part it scared him and in part he was as excited as a teenager in heat. He assumed the first blush would wear off at least sexually but they sure weren't there yet. He adjusted his pants and walked back to his office.

Later that afternoon, they reconvened. Mendez had given them nothing which wasn't surprising given his comatose state of the day of the murder. Torres not much more except to say that Pablo and José said almost nothing to each other the whole time Mendez and Torres were at the house on Desert Drive. In the same room except when one of them would go to the shed, or they were sharing drug paraphernalia, but no communication. Torres remembered thinking it was a bit odd but was scrambled himself enough not to pay a lot of attention to it. And no, he had never heard of a woman named Maria. He swore by the story about the TV.

Maria Thompson looked younger by years when Margaret got to the Center. There was some color in her face, her hair was washed and combed back, and she had lost some of the wariness that living on the streets seeps into the survivors. About a week after the first time with Pablo, she had gone to his room after José had fallen asleep and Pablo had given her the bottle then. She had put a little on that night while they had sex and then had washed it off before she went back to José's bedroom, a pattern she would follow until the night they were caught. Had José smelled the perfume when he broke into his brother's bedroom? No way to tell but she had put it on per their custom and the bottle was on the night stand. So maybe. She had never heard of Mendez and Torres.

Chapter Twenty Three

Busy Day at the Courthouse

On the following mid-November Tuesday, Jackie LaPointe walked a petition over to Probate Court asking the Probate Judge for Bernalillo County to have her named Guardian for Anthony Jiménez. Probate courts have jurisdiction over cases involving minors or people with disabilities and, because of Anthony's presumed handicaps, his lack of education and what had happened to him over his lifetime, his lawyers needed a Guardian appointed. The team had talked about whether the guardianship should be independent of the law firm but clearly Jackie was the only one that Anthony trusted. If a conflict of interest between the firm's role and Anthony's interest occurred, they would cross that bridge when they got to it.

On the same day, the firm filed Petitions with the same Probate Court to establish estates for Esther and Roberto Jiménez as well as Pablo Jiménez. This time they asked Peter Flemming, a long-time lawyer in Albuquerque who was in the twilight of his career, to act as the Personal Representative of the three estates. This all was a procedural necessity because if they were going to sue for money damages against dead people, they needed to have the estates formed.

The Probate Judge signed the order for the guardianship as well as the orders setting up the estates.

On the following day, Will Bennett filed a multi-count Complaint in Bernalillo County District Court on behalf of Anthony Jiménez against the three estates and José Jiménez claiming negligence, gross negligence, willful and wanton misconduct, intentional infliction of physical and emotional distress, assault and battery, and crimes against a disabled person. Rosalind, Jackie and Will had talked about the negligence count because what this family had done to Anthony wasn't anything like running a red light and causing an accident. The heart of the case of course were the intentional claims but they were hopeful that, by pleading negligence, they might find some insurance coverage from either a home owner's policy for the house or a renter's policy on the Jiménez apartment. Neither of the policies would cover intentional acts but they were hoping for at least some coverage.

The same day, Peter Flemming accepted service of the Complaint on behalf of the three estates and a process server served the papers on José Jiménez in jail. Just ahead of an Albuquerque Police detective serving an arrest warrant on José for the murder of his brother. As days go, this was not one of José's best.

Chapter Twenty Four

Respite

After the flurry of activity surrounding the filing of the pleadings on behalf of Anthony Jiménez and the filing of murder charges against José Jiménez, a lull hit. In the civil case against the estates and José, a period of time had to go by before Will could ask for a default judgment against the defendants if nobody filed an answer to the complaint and then begin to figure out how to get to what money there was in terms of the property and the life insurance policies. On the criminal side, José Jiménez had been arraigned and pled Not Guilty and the judge ordered that he be held in jail without bail. Rawlings had made the decision not to charge either Mendez or Torres as Accessories to Murder. It was going to be a difficult case just to make it stick to José and he thought adding the two other defendants just made it that much more difficult. And he had them on any number of drug related offenses that one, they weren't getting out of jail anytime soon and two, sooner or later the Public Defenders representing them would want to plead them out. The other thing he had going for the People of the State of New Mexico was that, even if José beat the murder charge, he also was going away for a very long time on running a meth house and on what charges Rawlings could bring for what José had done to Anthony.

In early December, several days before the deadline for defaulting the Defendants in the civil case, Will got a surprise call out of the blue from James (don't call me Jim) Flickinger, a well known defense attorney with one of the big Albuquerque firms. Shortly after Will had moved to New Mexico he had joined a defense firm and had represented Defendants in cases in which

Flickinger had represented a co-Defendant. Will had worked well with him and liked and respected him.

After an exchange of pleasantries, Flickinger got to the point.

"Will, I've just been retained to represent the Estates of Roberto and Esther Jiménez in the case you've filed. I may also be picking up the case against the brothers."

"How?"

"Home owners' insurance for the Desert Drive home. Negligence counts triggered the duty to defend. They're not paying a dime!" He was quick to add.

Bennett knew the distinction well having spent most of his career doing insurance defense work himself. If there were allegations of intentional misconduct as there certainly were here, the insurance company wouldn't be on the hook to pay for a verdict based on the misconduct but they would be on the hook for negligence if a jury were to find somehow that the Jiménez family was also negligent. But regardless, under New Mexico law, the insurance company had to provide a defense at least to the Estates of Roberto and Esther and were probably including the brothers as well to avoid to a default against them.

Will. "James, glad to have you in the fray. What can I help you with?

"For starters, how about an extension to answer your complaint and sort out who I'm representing?"

"Of course. How much time do you need?"

"Not sure. May need some days with the holidays coming up but I'll let you know and try to get it to you as soon as possible."

"That's fine. Oh, almost forgot to ask. Limits and carrier?" Tit for tat.

There was a noticeable pause at the other end.

"MISMO. $500,000."

Will had done work for MISMO both in Michigan and New Mexico.

"Give Mark Nelson my best." Nelson was the claims manager for the region and a straight shooter.

"I'll do that, Will. Look forward to working with you. Did I mention no payment on the intentional acts?"

"You're breaking up, James, I can barely hear you. Happy Holidays."

Will hung up. He now had potentially $2.4 million dollars in play. A good day.

The holidays in New Mexico are celebrated in high style with lots of parties and get togethers and the good restaurants were always packed. This year was no exception. The Albuquerque Police Department always has a party for its senior leadership and J.D. and Margaret used it as their 'coming out' party. There had been rumors afoot in both the homicide division and the district attorney's office but nothing concrete until the night of the party in the Hyatt ballroom downtown.

Margaret had gone shopping and showed up in a stunner of a dress that caused heads not just to turn but basically whiplash.

Her colleagues on the force had only known her in her professional capacity dressed well but always with a cut to her clothes that hid the shoulder holster and almost always without make up. This dress wasn't hiding much of anything and Margaret had taken great care to 'paint the corpse' as her great aunt had been fond of saying to highlight her high cheek bones and beautiful eyes. J.D. knew he had the most beautiful woman in the room on his arm and reveled in every minute of it. Once her fellow officers got over the shock, it became a beautiful evening of camaraderie and friendship fueled not just a little by the open bar. The couple Ubered home.

The last several weeks had continued to cement their relationship into something both realized was very precious especially where they were in life and every day each hoped that it would last forever. Work always a constant for both of them but now balanced with the knowledge they had somebody in their corner regardless of what life would throw at them. They hadn't actually moved in together and each was holding on to that slim remnant of independence but they were either at her place or his every night. Each other's clothes and toiletries were a permanent fixture in the other's.

For Will Bennett and the men and women of Johnston & Blackwell, the holidays were anything but a respite. For the business lawyers, year-end was always a time of stress because the books of their various business clients were getting ready to close and the litigators had never been busier. Year-end was always a push to resolve cases from the defense side and Will, Rosalind McManus, Luis Moreno and Jackie LaPointe were either in mediations or serious settlement discussions with the other side on any number of cases.

Between Jackie's work schedule and keeping track of Anthony Jiménez, little time was left over for her spouse,

Josephine Lucas. On the other hand, Dr. Lucas was busy in her own right as the youngest member of the anesthesia group at the University of New Mexico Hospital so time together was mighty precious. Still, they had each other and both of them were in awe that a chance meeting at a coffee shop would have come to this.

As for the case against the Jiménez estates and José, James Flickinger had appeared and filed an answer on behalf of all of the defendants under the theory that the assets that were available for sure like the property and the life insurance policies would be at risk if even one of the defendants were defaulted by the court for not answering the complaint. Flickinger and Will discussed what needed to be done to get the case ready for trial. For Will, the only statement under oath he needed was José Jiménez – everybody else was dead. He had also hired a national psychiatric expert on sexual abuse against people with disabilities. Her conclusion was that because the disabled are so much more vulnerable, the damage done is even worse and with near certainty is irreversible. Will had provided the report of Dr. Janis Davenport to Flickinger along with her resume and Flickinger saw no reason to go to the trouble of taking her statement under oath. It all made perfect sense to him.

Will had also had Anthony interviewed and tested by a local psychiatrist to try to come to a diagnosis. The best Dr. David Dowling could come up was that Anthony was on the spectrum of autism but both the interview and the testing were clouded by what the man child had suffered. There was one startling result of the testing that led Dr. Dowling to call Will at his office.

"Will, there's something you need to know about your client." Dramatic pause that caused Will to roll his eyes. "Anthony's IQ results are off the charts – like in the genius range."

Startled, "Are you sure?"

"No question. Every indicator I tested him on came back without fail. A real anomaly but there it is."

They rang off and Will sat in silence for a few minutes. The appearance of Anthony, his voice, his shyness, everything he'd been through…and he's a genius. He walked down the hall to Jackie's office.

"Dowling just called to tell me that Anthony's IQ results are in the genius range."

Jackie looked at him for a minute. "I guess I'm not surprised, Will. The more I get to know him and once you get past the obvious issues, there is something magical about him."

On his way back to his office, Will wondered whether he was smart enough to have killed his brother. He had been bothered by something for the longest time and couldn't ever quite get it into focus. But in his thoughts about Anthony's intelligence, it came to him. His business card. Anthony had told them that he had found it in the apartment after his dad had molested him but it had been found on Pablo's body. Had Mom and Dad taken more than one card the day they were at Will's office? Certainly possible and Will preferred that to any other answer but it still stopped him. He thought about mentioning it to Jackie and thought better of it at least for now. They had enough on their plates as it was.

As for Flickinger, the only statement he needed under oath was Anthony's. That had been on Will's and Jackie's minds since they had filed the case and neither was sure that Anthony could handle the stress. Nevertheless, it had to be done and Will and

James Flickinger had set aside two days in late January for it to get done.

Will had also considered the possibility of videotaping Anthony's trial testimony to play in front of the jury in place of Anthony actually testifying "live." If they were concerned about the stress of a statement under oath, what would being in a courtroom do to him? That decision was still on the table.

Christmas Eve, Alex and Will kept the night free for just the two of them at the townhouse – along with Josie and Jinks, the two black cats who ruled the household. Judge Kennedy had had her own year-end pressures as Chief Judge and welcomed the respite with just her husband. They each loved what they did for a living but this night they talked quietly about an end game. Will wondered aloud how long he could go on trying cases and Alex wondered aloud how long she truly wanted to be on the bench day in and day out making difficult decisions that impacted the lives of so many. Not to mention having to herd the other judges who were, in many ways, akin to a herd of cats. Christmas Day they slept in and when they got up, Will toyed with the idea of going into the office to clean up some loose ends but was quickly persuaded that there were better things to do with his wife than going to work. Turned out she was right.

Afterwards, they strolled over to the center of Old Town to see the luminarias on the ancient Catholic Church, got a bite to eat at one of the local Mexican restaurants, and then went back home. Will called his daughter, Grace, back in Michigan and caught up with her, comforted that she was happy and doing well and spending Christmas with her now longtime boyfriend, Jack Carter. Life was good and there was Peace on Earth.

That was about to change.

Chapter Twenty Five

Tenderloin

Across town, a Christmas afternoon snuggle with J.D. and Margaret was interrupted by Margaret's emergency number on her cell phone rang. She struggled off the couch, saw that it was the watch commander, and called him back.

"Another multiple homicide on east Central, Chief. Four dead this time from multiple gunshots, all women this time."

Margaret got the address, hung up, got her work clothes, and headed out the door, telling J.D. not to go anywhere with a blown kiss at the door. She activated her siren and her portable rooftop light and raced to the parking lot of the Starlighter 66 motel, a relic of glory days gone by that now was frequented by hourly guests. She arrived just ahead of the first television truck and found the parking lot filled with black and whites, lights flashing, and yellow tape around much of the second floor of the motel. She was met by Sergeant Jorge Rodruigez, the same officer who had been in charge of the scene at the Desert Drive murder.

"Merry Christmas, Jorge. We've got to stop meeting like this."

"This is a bad one, Margaret. One of them is ours."

Now stone serious, Margaret said, "Tell me."

"Since the first killings, Vice had been sporadically using undercover officers on east Central. Victoria Morrow was on duty this afternoon and apparently was responding to what were presumably gun shots coming from one of the second-floor rooms. She had her gun out but never had a chance. She's on the balcony.

We found another body closer to the stairs and two more in the room. Multiple gunshots, probably an assault rifle like the first ones."

There is nothing that chills a police officer more than to find out one of their own had been killed and Margaret Espinoza felt her throat go dry with dread.

"Witnesses?"

"Of course not. Never are."

"Desk clerk?"

Rodruigez looked at his notes. "Ben Livingston. Third day on the job so he drew Christmas. Rented Room 221 about three hours ago to a Caucasian male, maybe in his thirties, maybe older. Knit cap drawn over his forehead, couldn't tell color of hair, height somewhere between 5'8" and 6'2", average build, scar on the left side of his face. Matches about any white guy in New Mexico. Paid cash. Clerk never saw how he arrived or how he left."

"Compared to the description we got last time from the clerk?"

"Could be the same guy but with a description like that, who knows? We'll know for sure once we run ballistics."

"Morrow's gun?"

"May have gotten a shot off and we'll run that. Bullets damn near cut her in half, Chief."

Margaret nodded, put on some latex gloves, and headed up the stairs. Just at the top was a sheet covered body with a substantial amount of blood on the balcony floor. Farther down, a second sheet covered a body that Margaret knew was Morrow.

She stooped and lifted the sheet. She didn't recognize Victoria Morrow but it didn't matter. She had been one of them and the Chief of Homicide swore to herself that she would get the son of a bitch that had done this. She stood up and looked in Room 221. Crime scene officers were in the room and Margaret saw no reason to add to the confusion. She would know soon enough what they had found. She did note two other sheet covered bodies, one on a bed that had seen recent use and one nearer the door. A lot of blood. She retraced her steps to the parking lot, conferred briefly with the department's PR representative who would speak with the media, and then turned to see Randy Hilton, Chief of the ABQ Vice Squad, coming towards her.

"Victoria?"

Margaret nodded.

He bowed his head. "Fuck."

She nodded again.

She saw him take a deep breath, pull himself together, and head to the stairs.

Margaret stayed around the scene waiting for preliminary results from the crime scene investigators. She called J.D. and let him know she'd be a little longer and that one of the victims was a vice squad undercover officer.

"Fuck," he whispered and Margaret thought to herself that was as good a sentiment as any for a Christmas like this one. Dave Norton, head investigator, reported on his findings.

"Multiple casings and we're guessing it's the same gun as before. Probably sex so we'll have some DNA. Looks like he'd hired two of them like before. Each vic shot numerous times almost as though he was in some sort of rage. Lay opinion, Chief, but this is one sick asshole.”

“Thanks, Don.”

She found Jorge Rodriguez and confirmed there would be a police presence for the next 24 hours, then bone tired, she got back in her car and headed for home for a few hours’ sleep. She knew the next few days would be brutal. And they were.

Chapter Twenty Six

Media Frenzy

Margaret was in the office long before dawn getting updates from the crime scene people which was little more than she had gotten from Inspector Norton the night before. Early ballistics results established it was the same gun used last fall. The Medical Examiner had taken vaginal swabs from both of the victims in the room and had sent them for emergency DNA testing but if this was the same perp, he was wearing condoms and at best, the results would be inconclusive.

The best news was that Victoria Morrow had been able to get one shot off before she was killed and investigators had found a couple of blood spots on the balcony that they were hoping did not belong to the victims. Blood type would be huge.

One of her detectives came in with the early edition of the *Albuquerque Journal* with the lead headline that screamed **TENDERLOIN KILLER STRIKES AGAIN**. Fortunately, the media had not yet learned that one of the victims was a police officer. They would soon enough but at least this would give Officer Morrow's young family a chance to absorb the news in private.

At their place in Old Town, Will and Alex woke to the same headline. Some months ago, a sitting District Court judge, Donald Jenkins, had been outed by an anonymous caller and had been caught at the Starlighter not exactly with his pants down but close enough. He had been forced to resign. Will wondered idly if he was involved in this because once he was removed from the bench, he had made a successful living representing prostitutes and pimps. Maybe he knew something.

That thought had already occurred to Margaret and she was waiting for business to open to call him. In the meantime, she had filled in the Chief of Police who would be holding a press conference in a couple of hours. She very much admired and respected Chuck Dillard because he was a 'cop's cop.' Homegrown through the ranks, he had weathered some tough times leading the force through a federal investigation on police abuse and had never once wavered in his defense of his officers – to a fault some would say – but earning the respect of the rank and file along the way.

"So, Margaret, the usual bullshit? Interviewing witnesses, following leads, may well be the same killer, blah, blah, blah."

She smiled for the first time since her cell had gone off. "Yep, for now. But you should know that Victoria Morrow got a shot off before she died and we're hoping a couple of blood spots might be the perp's. Keep that under your hat for now."

"For sure. I'm going to announce one of the victims was an undercover officer. Randy has spoken with her husband. Two young kids. Arrangements pending. You'll be at the press conference?"

"Of course, Chief. See you there." She looked at her watch. Still an hour to go. She called Donald Jenkins' office and left a voice mail message to call her as soon as he could.

As press conferences go especially involving the Albuquerque Police Department, this was a muted affair as soon as Chief Dillard announced that one of the victims was an undercover police officer. Behind the Chief were Randy Hilton, Chief of Vice, who was clearly struggling with his emotions having just come from a meeting with Officer Morrow's family. Next to him was Chief of Homicide, Margaret Espinoza, who on the outside had her game face on but who, on the inside, was seething that she had an animal loose. She swore again she would bring him down.

The Chief took some questions from the press but stuck to the script. A couple of the reporters tried to push and the Chief had been around long enough and in front of the press long enough to push right back. At the end, it was almost anticlimactic with the Chief promising the force would do everything in their power to bring this murderer to justice.

Margaret got back to the office just in time to get the call from Donald Jenkins.

"Judge, thanks for calling me back."

"Not a judge anymore, Chief, but thanks for that."

She explained the purpose of her calling him wondering if, in his representation of clients associated with east Central, he had any sense of who might be behind these murders.

He thought for a moment. "I hear a lot of stuff from my clients, some of which I believe and some of which is obviously fantasy. There are certainly some vicious men out there who are physically abusive to the girls but I've never heard of anybody who actually wanted to kill them." Another moment. "But there is one guy who comes around every once in a while, who creeps the girls out. Always wears camouflage when he gets to east Central, gives orders in military speak, pays well, and then nobody sees him for weeks or months. Give me a couple of days to talk to some people."

"Thank you, Judge. That would be very very helpful."

"I'll do my best, Chief. I know the people who have been killed, represented some of them."

"Margaret."

"Don."

They hung up and Margaret wondered how many of the woman who had been killed had been more than clients. Whatever. That didn't matter. What mattered was that Donald Jenkins had just identified a 'person of interest.'

Chapter Twenty Seven

Requiem for a Cop

Any time a police officer is killed in the line of duty, the 'thin blue line' attends the memorial service or funeral sometimes from all across the country to honor their fallen and the memorial service for Victoria Morrow was no exception. Police departments from all over the Southwest sent contingents to the service and I-40 and I-25 were awash with police cruisers all heading to the service. Dressed in their finest blues, the officers lined the entrance to the church several hundred deep to pay homage to Victoria as her coffin passed.

Her parents, grandparents, sisters and brothers, and her husband and children followed the minister into the church and sat in the first pew. Off to the side the District and Metropolitan Judges led by Chief Judge Alexandra Kennedy sat together in their black robes. Chief Dillard spoke, Randy Hilton spoke, as did the minister. Victoria Morrow had always wanted to be a police officer, both her parents had been officers, and two of her siblings. She knew the dangers especially working Vice and she took it in stride, reveling in the adrenalin rush at the same time knowing she was doing something important to keep her community safe. She had paid the ultimate price.

The entourage to the cemetery spanned more than a mile with lights on the police cars following the hearse paying silent formal tribute to Victoria Morrow.

On the way back from the cemetery, Margaret Espinoza was uncharacteristically quiet and J.D. Rawlings was smart enough to let that be. She swore she would get the man who killed Victoria Morrow no matter how long it took and no matter what it took. He dropped her at her office and he went to his, agreeing

they would meet up at her place at the end of the day. The mood
in Homicide was somber – there was a cop killer on the loose and
the detectives intended to take him down.

Chapter Twenty Eight

Bad Days for Justice

The media coverage of the Tenderloin Killer was 24/7 on a national level and each day no progress was reported by the police department seemed to only add to the frenzy.

'Must be a slow news cycle,' Margaret thought to herself. Usually, sensationalist crimes had their 15 minutes of fame and then faded with the next random, senseless killing of innocent people. Maybe part of it was because the victims were prostitutes – there were plenty of Christian pastors opining this was God's way of punishing the women. And maybe it was because the police were saying nothing other than the usual 'leads are being pursued.' What the media didn't know was that there were leads being followed.

Don Jenkins had called back with a description of the man who had given some of the women the 'creeps.' In his late thirties/early forties, he was about 5'10", Caucasian, buzz cut hair style, very trim and muscular liked he worked out a lot, and a noticeable scar on his left cheek. He had told one of the women that his name was John Smith but that was certainly bogus. He would come to east Central maybe 6 or 7 times a year and always was dressed completely in camouflage although Jenkins' witnesses didn't know whether it was military or hunting dress. The police voted for military because each of the witnesses told Jenkins that they remembered that he spoke in very clipped tones and gave orders on what he wanted done as though he were in command of a military operation. He would arrive on foot, pick up women on the street corners, and then proceed to the Starlighter motel. If possible, he would always ask for Room 221. He always paid for the room in cash in advance and when he was done, he usually left a tip with the woman or women and then disappeared into the night. Nobody, of course, ever followed him although one woman remembered he headed west on Central and then turned north at the first intersection.

Margaret had asked Jenkins if she could interview the people he had talked to and he had told her that all of them had made it clear that they would only talk to him and not the police. He knew some of the names they used on the streets but they were bogus and he didn't even know the fictional names for some of them. She was unhappy with that but understood these women and the police were not exactly on a first name basis. She asked about a police artist and that also was declined. Jenkins did say that if the guy showed up again, the women and pimps were to call him immediately. That would have to do.

Based on what she had, she put out an All Points Bulletin to keep a look out for an individual matching the sketchy description and the police also added more patrols to east Central which, even though it was for the prostitutes' safety, caused a rather significant downturn in business. At best, a mixed blessing.

The crime people had identified the blood as Type AB, a rarity among blood types, and one that would be noteworthy if they could find the "person of interest." They had checked the various hospitals in the days after the killings and nobody had shown up with a gunshot wound that wasn't explained in some other way – drug deal gone bad, robbery with a gun, robbery with a gun except the victim had a bigger gun, the usual suspects. And none with Type AB blood. So if Morrow had shot him, it was either a flesh wound or he was self-medicating.

The homicide team led by Margaret had a working hypothesis that the perp was active or discharged military and the camouflage would have likely been either Army or Marines. The gun used in both attacks was the same – an AK47 that is not military issue but easy to come by in this country with or without background checks. Bullets were hollow points in both attacks designed to do the most damage possible on impact.

It was going to take a break to find this guy but the Albuquerque Police Department would never give up on a cop killer.

Meanwhile in late January at the Bernalillo County Courthouse, the case of the People of the State of New Mexico v. José Jiménez was getting underway with Judge Charles Peck presiding. There had been no discussions between the prosecutor's office and the public defender about a plea deal because there was no point. Regardless of the outcome, Jiménez was going away for a very long time based on the meth lab on the Desert Drive premises and the fact he was a habitual offender. The only difference was he had a chance of getting out as an old man without a murder conviction – with it, he was in for the duration.

It took almost a full first day to pick a jury with both J.D. Rawlings, for the prosecution, and Chris Patton, the public defender, questioning the various members of the jury pool on bias and prejudices and other individual experiences that might sway a juror one way or the other. The myth behind jury selection is that both sides are looking for truly impartial, neutral jurors who can listen to the facts and the law and come to a just verdict. The reality couldn't be more different – each side wants to pick a jury who will use their biases and prejudices to help the lawyer win the case. So the lawyers seesawed back and forth with Judge Peck giving them both leeway on their questioning and by 3:00 PM, they had 14 people in the jury box two of whom were alternates who would be dismissed before jury deliberations began. The judge swore the jury in and the trial was adjourned to the next morning with the usual cautionary instructions not to discuss the case with anyone or to do any independent research on the case, an instruction in the day and age of the internet and social media that was almost uniformly ignored.

The next morning Rawlings and Patton gave opening statements to the jury that were supposed to be 'road maps' on what the case looked like from the perspective of the prosecution and the defense. The themes were obvious.

After a particularly graphic description of the crime scene (with pictures no less), J.D. described the love triangle, the discovery by José that Maria Thompson was sleeping with his brother, the fight that night, and finally the murder. The conclusion? Only José Jiménez would have had the motive and the opportunity and only José in his rage would have mutilated Pablo's body as it was found. His weakness? The gun showed up at the murder/suicide of Roberto and Esther Jiménez when José Jiménez was already in jail.

Chris Patton was a good lawyer, was committed to being a Public Defender, and had tried a lot of cases. And he knew where his strengths and weaknesses were. His strengths? The prosecution couldn't put the murder weapon or at the scene, for one, and two, when José found out about Pablo and Maria, why did he wait weeks to kill him? His weaknesses? Who the hell else would have done this?

Once the jury had been picked, the case itself took only two days to try. Rawlings put on the investigating police officers, the crime scene detectives, the medical examiner and the pathologist who did the autopsy. Several of the jurors winced at the testimony about the perfume bottle. As to those witnesses who were at the scene, Patton's cross examination was short and to the point. To each of them, he asked whether they had seen any evidence of the gun at the scene. Rawlings ended his case with the testimony of Maria Thompson who described her relationship first with José and then with Pablo and then the night Maria and Pablo had been discovered and the fight that ensued. Patton's cross? He went into much detail how Maria Thompson had lived her life on the streets attacking her credibility and then had her agree that when she left the house after the fight, both brothers were still alive.

After the prosecution rested its case, Chris Patton rested his case for the defense without calling a witness. It wasn't a close call for him. To put José Jiménez on the stand would be a disaster and the jury would be told that they couldn't hold the fact that the defendant didn't testify against him.

Closing arguments, the afternoon of the third day, mirrored the themes from the opening statements as well as the testimony of the witnesses. Rawlings made the point that because the gun had Esther's fingerprints on it, she could have come to the house and retrieved it but even J.D. knew the timing didn't work between the 911 call and the discovery of the body and the arrival of the first police officers unless the gun had been hidden in such a way that only Esther would have known where to find it.

Chris Patton's closing argument started with a line, as a Public Defender, he had used many times.

"Ladies and gentlemen, I'm guessing from what you have heard over the past days, you don't much like my client." Patton looked back at José Jiménez at counsel table and then turned back to the jury. "Frankly, I don't like him much myself. But that doesn't make him a murderer. And here's why."

He went on to concede that José had motive and opportunity but without the means - the gun, the jury had to find him not guilty because the prosecution hadn't proven its case beyond a reasonable doubt. He described the theory that the mother had come in later and removed the gun from a secret hiding place as 'rank speculation' and sat down with these final words to the jury.

"You don't have to like José Jiménez but you must find him not guilty of his brother's murder. José and I will be waiting for your verdict."

The jury received the instructions from the judge on the law that they must follow in their deliberations and then excused them for the night with the warning that they were not to talk about the case with anyone including family members, were not to watch media coverage of the trial, and were not to use the internet or social media to discuss the case. Even as he said it, everybody in the courtroom knew exactly what would happen as soon as the jurors got home: they'd tell their family all about it, turn on the TV to see if it had made the news, and surf the internet for information about the case. Human nature.

That night Margaret and J.D. went to the Monte Carlo for drinks and dinner. Even in a relatively short trial like this one, J.D. was exhausted but happy it was over. He had put on the best case he could but knew the jury would have to make a leap of faith to get to a guilty verdict. Margaret had sat in on some of the testimony and the closing arguments and had thought, regardless of the outcome, her lover had been a stunning advocate. She had seen him in trial before of course but only as a witness and not as a spectator and she had loved the way he commanded the attention of both the judge and jury. She also had to begrudgingly admit that Chris Patton was a worthy adversary and that it was a close call. Wisely, J.D. let Margaret drive him home and put him to bed. When she got back from the bathroom, he was already sound asleep. She crawled in next to him, her last thoughts not on the trial but what the rest of her life might look like with J.D. Rawlings. It didn't scare her anymore.

Dawn came early and J.D. was up and showering seemingly no worse the wear for the night before. He went to the courthouse and was at counsel table when the jury was escorted into the courtroom. The judge gave some brief instructions and sent them to the jury room to deliberate. Rawlings and Patton went back to their respective offices to wait for the verdict.

At 3:30 PM, the bailiff called and said the jury had reached a verdict. Patton and José were at the defense table and Rawlings at his.

The bailiff. "All rise." Everybody stood and Judge Peck entered and instructed the bailiff to get the jury. They followed the bailiff in and took their seats.

The judge. "Would the foreperson please rise?"

A middle-aged man stood up.

"Have you reached a verdict, Mr. Foreman?"

"We have, Your Honor."

"What is it?"

"We find the defendant not guilty."

It was almost as though somebody let the air out of the courtroom.

"So say you all?"

Each juror affirmed that indeed was their verdict.

The judge thanked the jury for their service and excused them.

"Anything further, counsel?"

Almost in unison, Rawlings and Patton said, "No, Your Honor."

"All right. The prisoner will be returned to jail to await proceedings on the other pending charges." Jiménez was led out of the courtroom by sheriff's deputies.

"Gentlemen, it has been a pleasure to have two fine advocates like yourselves in front of me. I'm not sure justice was done but that's not a topic for discussion now. Congratulations on a job well done. We're adjourned."

After the judge left the bench, Patton and Rawlings shook hands and told each other they had tried a good case. They knew each other well, had tried numerous cases against each other, and had great respect one for the other.

Rawlings packed his briefcase and went back to the office at least somewhat mollified by the fact that Jiménez had so many other charges against him, it would be a very long time before he saw freedom again. And then a fleeting thought. 'If it wasn't José, who?'

That night Margaret and J.D. ordered in Chinese at Margaret's place. After a second glass of wine was poured, J.D.

posed the question he had been asking himself, "If not José, who?" Margaret thought for just a minute. "Well, I still like José even if he was found not guilty. There are several ways that gun disappeared. You just couldn't prove it beyond a reasonable doubt. Sure as hell doesn't mean he didn't do it. I mean jamming a broken perfume bottle up the poor kid's ass. Only somebody as mean as José would do something like that."

J.D. nodded absently and went back to work on the sweet and sour chicken.

That night just before she went to sleep, Margaret had a random thought. Anthony?

The next morning, she was up early and off to the office. Since the trial had been going on, her detectives had scoured the East Central area for a man answering the description, albeit generic, of the 'person of interest' but the trail had gone very cold. Nobody had seen anybody in the area matching the description and Margaret wasn't surprised. Knowing he had killed a cop, that would be the last place the man would go. They continued to check with local hospitals and clinics and also had officers at the train station and the airport but other than the scar on the left cheek, there was little to distinguish him. And not having even an artist's sketch wasn't helping. Hair could grow, beards could grow to cover the scar among other problems facing the police. Margaret was becoming increasingly pessimistic about finding Victoria Morrow's murderer.

Chapter Twenty Nine

Across the Way

The same day, the jury returned a verdict of not guilty in the José Jiménez trial, Anthony Jiménez was to give his statement right under oath in the civil case that had been brought against his parents' estates, his brother Pablo's estate, and José. Jackie and Will had debated long and hard on how much to prepare Anthony for his statement – it ran the whole gamut from videotaping in role play to mock cross examinations to Will's favorite: 'Tell the truth briefly.' They agreed on the latter and spent very little time with Anthony ahead of the event.

Shortly before 10:00 AM, James Flickinger, the defense lawyer looking like he'd rather be anywhere than where he was, and the court reporter showed up at Johnston & Blackwell with one other person in tow. She was introduced as Annette Miller, Senior Claims Adjuster for MISMO Property and Casualty Insurance Company, the homeowner's insurance carrier for the Jiménez parents. Flickinger asked if she could sit in and Will and Jackie agreed. Introductions were made and everybody was shown into the conference room.

The court reporter asked Anthony Jiménez to raise his right hand.

"Do you swear or affirm to tell the truth, the whole truth and nothing but the truth?"

"*I do.*" He held Jackie's hand tightly.

Flickinger: "Would you state your full name for the record?"

"Anthony Jiménez."

For the next 45 minutes, Flickinger asked a series of questions about Anthony's experiences at the hands of his parents and his brothers. In a frightening emotionless monotone, Anthony answered the questions directly and without guile. At the end of that time, Flickinger asked to have a brief recess and he and Ms. Miller went out into the hallway. The court reporter asked to be excused and left the room with tears in her eyes. Will, Jackie and Anthony sat in silence with Anthony's hand securely in Jackie's. When they reassembled and went back on the record, Flickinger said simply: "I have nothing further. Thank you, Mr. Jiménez."

"You're welcome." And it was done.

As they packed up to leave, Will was sure he saw tears in Flickinger's eyes. Miller was stoic. The court reporter was sobbing.

After they left, Jackie asked, "Anthony, are you OK?"

"I want to go home now, Jackie."

"OK, let's get your coat and go home."

After they left, Will looked at his watch. It wasn't quite 11:00. 'Probably too soon to start drinking' he said to himself 'even by my standards.' He breathed a huge sigh of relief and went back to his office marveling at how damaged the young man was and how poised he was throughout the statement. Then a random thought. Was Anthony capable of killing?

It was a question he repeated to himself when he heard about the verdict in the Pablo Jiménez murder trial.

Chapter Thirty

A Break

Two days after the Jiménez verdict, the detectives caught a major break in the Morrow cop killing. A few days after Victoria Morrow was shot and killed, a burglary had been reported at an urgent care center in a strip mall eight blocks north of Central Ave. It was a seedy part of town and the investigating officers had assumed that the motive was money because both the back door and the cash drawer had been jimmied open and about $1,500 in small bills had been taken. The center had no alarm system so the break-in hadn't been noticed until the next morning when the first shift showed up for work. The officers made short work of their visit there, filled out the requisite forms, and went on about their day with the near certainty that it was another petty crime that would never be solved.

But that afternoon, Burglary got a call from the administrator of the center, a Shirley Evans, indicating that it appeared as though additional things had been taken, things that immediately sparked the interest of the Duty Officer and that prompted a call to the Homicide Division. What was missing were medical supplies: gauze bandages, alcohol wipes, a bottle of alcohol, antibiotic cream, suture material, and surgical tape. The administrator was told to immediately close off the room where the supplies had been stored and Margaret Espinoza ordered a crime scene crew to the scene at the same time grabbing her gun and coat off the chair and heading for the exit.

She beat the crime investigators by minutes and then waited impatiently for the preliminary results. She had that same intuitive feeling she had had before – that this was the break they had been waiting for. She wasn't disappointed. Sergeant Andrea Budo, in charge of the team, came out to report to Margaret. She confirmed what they already knew about the missing supplies but added a blockbuster while barely able to keep her game face on.

"We think we may have found some blood spots on the floor by the cabinet where the supplies were taken. Got swabs and will get back to you still this afternoon with the preliminary results."

Margaret kept her game face on as well but felt the surge of excitement.

"Make sure you run what you have here with what we found at the Starlighter, Sergeant."

She didn't see it but Budo gave the Chief of Homicide a look like: 'just how dumb do you think we are?' But she nodded her assent and a few minutes later left with her team. Margaret thanked the administrator and asked her some questions about some of the patients. Had she ever seen anyone who favored military fatigues, had a buzz cut, Caucasian, and had a prominent scar on his left cheek. The woman couldn't think of anybody that matched anything like the description, but indicated she would check with the nurses, aides, and doctors and report back if anything positive came of it. Espinoza nodded and said that she might well send out a detective to follow up as well. She could tell Evans wasn't too keen on the idea given patient privacy issues but when Margaret told her who they were looking for, a murderer six times over and a cop killer, she relented.

"Some of those women he killed came here for care, Detective. We'll help any way we can."

Late that afternoon, Budo called Espinoza and almost shouted,

"It's a match, Margaret. It's a fucking match. A couple of more tests that will take a day or two but I am 99.99% sure. I'd bet my badge on it."

Quietly. "Thank you, Sergeant. Excellent work."

She hung up and sat quietly for a few moments. Part of her wanted to feel the excitement that Budo felt. But what she really felt was an overwhelming rage at a world that would allow vermin like this to exist. She thought of Morrow's kids and her own son and tears came to her eye. Senseless. Awful. Final.

It had been eight days since the murders and the killer had gone to ground presumably for that whole period of time. Wherever Morrow had shot him, it was serious enough not to have healed over if he was still dropping blood at the urgent care center and that meant a couple of things. He had to be getting weak from loss of blood and he had to be desperate to break into the center, try to pass it off as a robbery, and be there mainly for the medical supplies. The suture material interested her. Did he have some sort of medical background or did he know the only way he was going to stop the bleeding was with stitches?

On the one hand, if he is this seriously wounded, they could just wait him out and assume he would die and somebody would find him. On the other hand, she wanted him badly. Really badly.

Margaret called in Detectives Bunker and Anderson, laid out what she had, and made the plan to traverse the neighborhood surrounding the urgent care center with what they had by way of description. They chose to use uniformed officers because of the nature of the crime and she thought the residents would be more responsive to "boots on the street" than plain clothes detectives. Lastly, she called Chief Dillard and filled him in. Turned off her light and headed to J.D.'s place.

Chapter Thirty One

Takedown

J.D. and Margaret both had too much on their plates to do much other than J.D. stopping at their favorite pizza place for a take home, a couple of glasses of wine, and then to bed. Margaret thought for a moment that maybe the bloom was coming off but it was the last conscious thought she had before falling asleep. That night, she had lots of jangled dreams, lots of running but she couldn't tell if it was to something or from something. Guns and gun shots in some of them and, at one point, J.D. woke her out of one of the nightmares worried she was going to kick him hard enough to do bodily harm.

Morning came early. Coffee and a bagel on the run and they were out the door back to the jungles they called careers.

"Hope you get him today, love."

"Thanks. Me too."

"Shoot straight." He winked and got into his car and drove out the driveway.

She followed. 'Shoot straight' and her thoughts returned to her dreams.

It wasn't fifteen minutes after she got in the door that her phone rang.

"Espinoza."

"Shirley Evans, Detective. Good morning. I have some news."

Margaret waited in silence.

"One of our Nurse Practitioners remembers a patient who matches your description." A pause as Evans looked at something. "He was in 10 days ago with a bronchitis. First time patient. She remembers the fatigues, the buzz cut, and the scar. We fixed him up with some antibiotics and sent him home to come back in 48 hours for a checkup and he never came back."

'That's because in the meantime he had killed several more victims and Victoria Morrow had shot him' Margaret thought to herself.

"Name?"

Another pause. "Desmond Allen." Evans didn't wait for the next question. "1342 Bristol Northeast, Apartment 412."

Margaret put the address about three blocks from the urgent care center.

"Ms. Evans, I can't thank you enough for your help. It means the world to us."

"Hope he's your man, Detective. People like him don't deserve to live."

They hung up and Margaret thought about what to do next. By the book, she should be getting search warrants and a SWAT Team gearing up. But there were two problems with that. One, it wasn't a slam dunk that Desmond Allen was the killer. Hell, half the men in Albuquerque wore camo and had scars and that generic a description might not satisfy a judge to issue a warrant. Two, it would take time and given how seriously Allen was injured, time was in short supply if she wanted him alive. And she did. So she made a command decision that would later earn her a thirty day paid suspension and an under the table citation for bravery above and beyond the call of duty.

She decided to go rogue and go it alone. She made certain her service-issued Glock was locked and loaded, she got her ankle gun strapped on, and got the long knife she had inherited from her grandfather from the locked lower drawer of her desk and hung the sheath on her belt under her blazer. As normal as possible, she opened her office door and announced – perhaps a tad too loudly – that she was going out to get a Starbucks and would be back shortly. When she got to the garage, she opened the trunk of her car, took her blazer off, and put on her Kevlar vest. Took a deep breath, pulled out of the garage and headed for Apt. 412, 1342 Bristol Northeast.

The building itself took up half the block, dirty red brick, five stories high, and clearly had seen better days. Probably post World War II and not much had been done to it since it had opened. The neighborhood matched the strip mall where the urgent care center was located and Margaret had a fleeting thought marveling at the men and women who worked the long hours to bring health care to the poor people of this neighborhood. As she looked the building over, she wondered whether some of the victims had lived here and whether there had been some connection between the victims and Allen before their deaths. It would be something to check on down the line – assuming there was a 'down the line.'

She walked up to the main door that entered into a foyer with names and buttons on the left ahead of a door that went into the main building. She tried it on the off chance it was broken but no such luck. She rang the manager's bell and an old voice answered.

"Yes?"

"Albuquerque Police, ma'am. Please open the door."

There was a pause and Margaret thought maybe the manager would ignore her. But the buzzer rang and she opened the door. The door to Apartment 102 opened just a crack with the chain still in place and a wizened face peered out. Margaret flashed her badge.

"Just a routine call, ma'am. Shouldn't take long at all."

There are two kinds of people in the world. Those who have all kinds of questions when the police show up, want to see warrants, badges and a bunch of other stuff. Then there is the other group who shrugs its shoulders and figures if it doesn't have anything to do with them, so be it. This manager clearly fell into the latter group, she nodded, and closed the door. Margaret heard the dead bolt slide into place. She could only wonder where the help came from when a toilet overflowed. It looked to her like tenants here were pretty much left to their own devices.

It was a walk up and four floors later, she thanked the time she had spent working out at the police gym. Even so at the top of the landing on the fourth floor, she paused to catch her breath. From the time the manager's door had closed to now, there had not been a sound from any of the apartments on any of the floors – no music, no babies, no smell of food cooking, nothing. Odd. She found Apt. 412 half way down the hallway, pulled the Glock, switched off the safety, and knocked on the door. No answer. Knocked again and no answer. She tried the door and it was locked. One of the many things Margaret Espinoza had learned over the years was that most locks in old apartment buildings were made to be picked. She had her kit with her but thought she'd try the credit card first. She slid it down the space between door and

jamb and the door swung open. No sense worrying about not
having a warrant when she could always say she'd been invited in.

She stepped into the smell of death everywhere. She could
smell blood but also rot and decay. It's hard to explain the smell
of death and dying but those who have witnessed it and smelled it
never forget it. Past the small entry, she walked into the living
room, gun raised, and saw a man in the only chair in the room, an
overstuffed purple chair that looked as though it had been there
ever since 1342 Bristol Northeast had been built. He fit the
description, buzz cut, cheek scar, fatigues. His eyes were half
open as he looked her over. She saw an Army issue .45 caliber
hand gun on the stand next to him.

His fatigues were blood stained with most of the blood
centered on a dirty white towel that he was holding in his crotch
with both hands.

'Oh my God. Victoria, you shot him in the crotch.' Even
with the drama of the moment, Margaret almost couldn't suppress
a smile. 'You go, girl.'

"Mr. Allen, my name is Detective Margaret Espinoza and I
am Chief of the Homicide Division of the Albuquerque Police
Department. You are under arrest for the murder of Officer
Victoria Morrow as well as a number of women killed at the
Starlighter Motel on East Central.

She saw the recognition in his eyes and she knew there was
no mistake that Desmond Allen was a/k/a 'John Smith.' She was
equally certain she would find the gun that had killed the women
someplace in the apartment. A wave of pain crossed over his eyes
and she wondered how much time he had left. Not much.

"Mr. Allen, you are a sick, fucking pervert, no better than a rat in the sewer living on garbage and looking for something to sink its teeth into. You are vermin who never deserved to be born and never deserved to live. If you served your country in the military, my guess is you were as big a yellow-bellied cock sucker as you are now. You make me sick. Here's your choice, asshole, you're going to pick that .45 up beside you, put the barrel in your mouth, and pull the trigger. If you don't, I'm going to put on these latex gloves and do it for you. Makes no difference to me. But here's the one thing. If I do it, before I leave, I'm ripping that towel off what's left of your dick, take some pictures, and post them at the Police Department in honor of Victoria Morrow and what she did to you in the seconds before she died. The other place I'm going to put them is in the lobby of the Starlighter Motel to remind patrons what happens to Johns who use violence and death to pleasure themselves. Your call."

It was the longest speech Margaret Espinoza had ever made.

Allen took a long time and lifted his right hand to the table and picked up the gun. The detective stood her ground with the Glock aimed at his forehead and if the barrel moved toward her, she would end it. She didn't have to. Desmond Allen put the barrel in his mouth and pulled the trigger, the force of the shot spraying brain matter onto the wall behind him. He didn't want to be shot by a woman, of all people, who called him a 'yellow-bellied cock sucker.' He couldn't abide that. He would do it himself.

She took a deep breath, walked over to the body, pulled the towel away, muttered 'Forgive me, Father, for I have sinned," and took several pictures with her phone of the mutilation that Victoria had accomplished in the last seconds of her life. The pictures would find their way to exactly where she had told Allen they wouldn't. 'Hey, what's a little white lie with a cop killer?'

She stepped back, called and waited for back up, knowing the shit storm would begin as soon as Chief Dillard found out what his Chief of Homicide had done on the rogue.

She sat on the 4th Floor landing step waiting for reinforcements. She started to laugh. 'Jesus, Victoria, you shot his balls off and he held on to what was left of his crotch for 10 days. Woman, talk about leaving your mark!' She was still smiling to herself when the black and whites arrived, sirens and lights ablaze with an urgency they didn't need. It was over. Forever.

Over the next 24 hours, there was indeed a shit storm on several fronts. Margaret was suspended with pay for 30 days, there was a party for her the night after Allen's death that included the entire homicide division and Chief Dillard. At the party the Chief gave her a "confidential" citation for bravery, the Albuquerque media outlets were awash with praise for her, and the crime scene team found the AK47 in Allen's apartment that was the weapon used in the Starlighter killings.

Two other items of note occurred within the days after the shooting. A small plaque was anonymously set next to Victoria Morrow's tombstone that said simply: 'You got your man. RIP.' And J.D. Rawlings proposed to Margaret Espinoza. She said yes.

Chapter Thirty Two

Anthony

Two months went by, it was early April in Albuquerque, and Will Bennett was preparing for the Anthony Jiménez trial. The defense had suggested mediation in which the parties get together with either a mediator or a former judge and try to resolve their differences short of actually going to trial. It was an unmitigated disaster and, to Will, was a massive waste of time and money. He was there with Anthony and Jackie LaPointe as Anthony's Guardian and on the other side, Peter Flemming was there as the Personal Representative of the Estates of Robert and Esther Jiménez and Pablo Jiménez and José, James Flickinger representing the defendants, and Annette Miller on behalf of MISMO, the home owner's insurance company. Will demanded the MISMO policy limits and the house and property at 1305 Desert Drive. Ms. Miller took the position that there was no insurance coverage because these were intentional acts not covered by the policy and Flickinger took the position that neither José, since moved to prison, nor Esther's sisters, the only other heirs, would agree to give up their interests to Anthony even though he likewise was an heir.

Shortly before lunch, Will asked to see Flickinger by himself and exploded.

"Why the hell did you think mediation was such a good Goddamned idea when you show up and offer nothing?"

"Will, I am so sorry. I had had conversations with Miller that I thought were going somewhere but I guess somebody at home office got a burr under their saddle and refused to offer anything. For whatever it's worth, I think she feels badly about showing up with no money."

"Oh right, James. Because insurance adjusters always feel badly when they're not paying. Well, Anthony can't take Ms. Miller feeling badly to the bank so we're out of here. See you in court." And was immediately chagrinned as he had sworn to himself he would never, ever say something that stupid.

Anthony, Jackie and Will said their goodbyes to the mediator and headed back to the office.

When they got back there was a message to see Liz LaRue right away. She found Will and asked to see him alone. They went into his office and she closed the door.

"Just got a call from Rawlings' office. José Jiménez was gang raped yesterday and stabbed to death. According to J.D.'s assistant, it went on for a long time." Liz turned around and left.

He felt nothing.

Will walked down to the conference room where Anthony and Jackie and said simply that José had died. Silence.

"Good."

And Will, always the lawyer, thought to himself there's one less obstacle in the way to Anthony at least getting the house and property…if they got a judgment.

"Jackie, would you open an Estate for José, substitute it in for him personally and we'll use Flemming for this one as well."

"On it, Chief." She saluted and Anthony laughed. "Let's get you home, sport."

"Okey dokey artichokey." He laughed again and this time they joined him. 'Maybe he's going to be OK after all.'

The next weeks went by quickly as final preparations for trial kicked into high gear.

Will and Jackie had also filed a lawsuit against the life insurance company for failing to pay Anthony on the two $500,000 policies because he wasn't named as a beneficiary. That case had just improved a tad with the news of José's death but was still an uphill battle trying to convince a judge to give $1,000,000 to an heir who hadn't been named even as a contingent beneficiary. That one would have to wait for this one to be over.

A week before trial, Will got a call from James Flickinger.

"Will, I'm embarrassed beyond words to make this call but have to."

"'Sup?"

"MISMO has authorized me to offer you $15,000 to settle the case against all of the defendants."

Silence. Will almost said 'see you in court' but caught himself in time.

"I'll pass it on, James, but I'm pretty sure I know the answer."

"Me too. Sorry, Will. I'm sick about this, you know that, don't you?"

"We all are. See you next week."

After they hung up, Will passed the offer on to Jackie as Anthony's Guardian who promptly turned it down. They talked about Flickinger's 'rock and a hard place' issue that Will, as a former defense lawyer, knew all too well. Flickinger had been retained by MISMO to represent the defendants under a home owner's policy on the Desert Drive address. He hadn't put up much of a battle because there wasn't much of a battle to put up given the uncontroverted testimony. But the ace in the hole for MISMO was that if all Will could do was prove intentional acts against Anthony's parents and brothers, there was an exclusion in the policy for intentional acts and MISMO wouldn't have to pay anything. On the other hand, if he could convince the jury that there was also negligence on the part of especially the parents, then there would be insurance and MISMO would have to pay the verdict up to the limits of liability of $500,000. That was the challenge.

That afternoon, Will sent a letter offering to settle the case within the policy limits of MISMO's $500,000 home owner's policy. He did it to preserve the potential to pursue a bad faith claim against MISMO if he could get a jury to bite on the negligence theory.

Bases covered, the team waited for Monday's start.

Chapter Thirty Three

Trial

The weekend was spent preparing Anthony for his testimony. Jackie and Will had again thought about videotaping and role playing but decided, once again, that the more they prepared their star witness, the more it might unnerve him. Instead, they spent the time talking about the events that had gone on for so long, going over his statement under oath, and making certain they had the right clothes laid out for him.

Late Sunday afternoon, Will asked, "Anthony, are you ready?"

Holding Jackie's hand, he said simply, *"Yes, Will."*

Monday morning and Will, Jackie and Anthony entered the courtroom and set up at the plaintiff's counsel table. Shortly after their arrival, James Flickinger walked into the courtroom with Peter Flemming, as the Personal Representative of the various estates, by his side. Behind the bar that separated the spectators from the lawyers and the judge, Will recognized Annette Miller from MISMO on one of the benches. Wisely, she sat on the plaintiff's side of the spectator section so as not to be too obvious as to who she was.

Judge Charles Peck entered the Second Judicial District Courtroom at exactly 8:30 AM, asked if there were any preliminary matters, and, hearing none, asked the bailiff, Manny Becerra, to bring the members of the jury pool into the courtroom. Approximately 50 men and women were escorted in and took their seats in the pews of the spectator section. Both sides had gotten the questionnaire answers from each of the prospective jurors so had some sense of who the people were. From Will's perspective, because it was such a horrible story, he wasn't as concerned about who ultimately actually sat on the jury. His wish list would include somebody who had experience with home owners' insurance but that wasn't likely to happen given that Flickinger would kick the person off in a heartbeat. Judge Peck gave a short speech to the entire group telling them that this was a civil case and that the Plaintiff was suing for damages arising out of alleged assaults by his parents and brothers. There was at least one audible gasp from the group and all eyes looked at the back of the head of Anthony Jiménez.

The Judge asked the potential jurors some preliminary questions and then turned the questioning over to Will. He briefly outlined the case and several of the jurors looked over at Anthony, sitting stoically at counsel table holding Jackie's hand. By the time Will was done with his questions, two of the women and one of the men had tears in their eyes. 'They'll do' he said to himself as he sat down.

James Flickinger got up, introduced himself, introduced Peter Flemming, and explained who he was and why he was there. He asked one question: "Can each of you listen to the evidence, put aside your sympathies, and decide the case fairly?" Which from Will's perspective was about the silliest question in the world to ask. What the hell were they going to say: "No?" Except much to his surprise, the three who had had tears in their eyes, shook their heads. Flickinger followed up and each potential juror said they could not be fair given what they knew about the case. Judge Peck weighed in with his own questions.

"Ladies and gentleman, given that this is indeed a very tragic story, as I'm sure everyone can agree, are you at least able to keep an open mind and listen to the evidence and listen to each other in the jury room?”

Each reluctantly nodded their heads ‘yes.’

“Anything further, Counsel?”

“No, your Honor.” Flickinger knew when the case first came in the door that, one, he was going to have to try it and two, he was going to hate every minute of it. He mentally wondered how long before he could retire.

“Gentlemen, let’s go into my chambers.” Will and James followed the judge and the court reporter into the judge’s chambers, and each of them lined up the seating charts they had for the potential jurors.

“Mr. Bennett, any challenges for cause?

“No, Your Honor.”

“Mr. Flickinger, any additional challenges for cause?”

“Yes, Your Honor, move to excuse for cause Jurors 12, 23, and 47.”

“Denied. Mr. Bennett, any preemptory challenges?”

“No, Your Honor, Plaintiff is satisfied with the panel.”

“Mr. Flickinger?”

“Yes, your Honor. Defendants strike Jurors 12, 23, and 47.” The same three he couldn’t get excused for cause.

They all trooped back to the courtroom. Judge Peck called the names of each of the people selected as jurors and the alternates and they took their places in order in the jury box, some with an expression of interest and curiosity and some with a sour expression that read 'bad luck.'

Judge Peck swore the jury panel in and called for a short recess before initial instructions and opening statements. Will sat at counsel table going over his notes one more time. Oblivious to everything but the task at hand, Will failed to take notice that several members of Johnston & Blackwell had come over to watch and had also failed to notice the Chief Judge of the Second Judicial District Court, Alexandra Kennedy, also enter and take a seat in the back row of the courtroom.

The bailiff, Manny Becerra, entered the courtroom, said "All Rise" and Judge Peck entered from his chambers and took the bench. "Please be seated. Counsel, anything further before Mr. Becerra brings the jury in?"

"No, your Honor." In unison.

"Mr. Becerra, please bring the jury in."

A moment passed. The door from the jury room opened and the eight jurors entered the courtroom and took their assigned seats. After reading the initial instructions to the jury giving them the rules to follow during the course of the trial, Judge Peck looked at Will.

"Mr. Bennett, are you ready to proceed with your opening statement?"

"Yes, Your Honor."

Without a note, Will walked to the podium with the welcome feeling of the adrenaline rush he hoped he would never lose. He took a deep breath, looked each juror in the eye, and began.

"Lost and alone. Lost and alone and tortured by those who should have loved him unconditionally. And that's why we're here. To get justice for what was done to Anthony Jiménez."

While opening statements are meant to be statements of fact and not conclusions such as a lawyer can use in closing arguments, there is a well-worn axiom that a little argument especially at the beginning is excusable and hence the 'lost and alone' theme.

Will went on for the next twenty minutes cataloguing the horrors upon horrors perpetrated on Anthony because he was too weak and too challenged to be able to fight back. He also concentrated on the issue of the negligence of the parents in leaving Anthony with his brothers after they moved away from the home into the apartment knowing full well what was going to happen to Anthony after they left him at their mercy.

The third time Will used the word 'negligence' it drew an objection from James Flickinger on the grounds that it was argument and conclusory…which it was. Judge Peck sustained the objection but the point had been made that there was a negligence claim against the parents that, if found by the jury, would trigger the home owners' insurance. Everybody except the jury knew exactly what Will was doing and Flickinger had weighed letting it go rather than bring it to the jury's attention like the 'unrung bell' but finally had to put a stop to it because he knew Will would keep pushing it until the judge stopped him.

"Ladies and gentlemen, for most of the testimony from the experts, I am going to ask Anthony to step away from the courtroom and not be present. He has been through enough. But he will testify and you will hear firsthand what he went through. At the end of this trial, after you have heard from the people who have treated Anthony and who have loved him for the first time in his life, I will be back to ask you for the justice he so deserves."

He took a moment and looked each juror. Each looked back. He nodded his head and returned to counsel table. There was not a sound in the courtroom for what seemed like forever.

Judge Peck cleared his throat. "Mr. Flickinger, do you wish to make an opening statement?"

"Yes, Your Honor." He walked to the podium with one page of notes. "Ladies and gentlemen, I don't condone what went on here and neither does Mr. Flemming, the Personal Representative of the estates of Mr. Jiménez's parents and his brothers. All of them are dead and they have paid the ultimate price, in one fashion or another, for what they did to their son and their brother. I can only hope that if they were still here, they would beg Anthony for forgiveness." He sat down.

Will looked at the jury and their body language and it was clear they were having none of the 'beg for forgiveness' argument. And Will knew that Flickinger knew that as well but what the hell, he had to say something.

Will's first witnesses were the first responders to the 911 call at 1305 Desert Drive. They described the scene of chaos, the location of the murder victim, and the condition of the three men in the living room. Lunch break. After lunch came the crime scene investigators who discovered the shed with the filthy mattress and shreds of clothing and the meth lab at the back of the property. Will then called the Chief of Homicide, Margaret Espinoza, who confirmed much of what had already been gone over but specifically talked about the dead bolt lock on the inside of the shed and the sense of movement she had seen on her second visit to the property.

She also testified to going to the home of the parents of the dead young man to tell them what had happened. Over objection by the defense lawyer, she testified that in her experience, it seemed as though Roberto and Esther were both not surprised by the news and even somehow knew it would ultimately come to this end.

For Will, this was critical testimony to the negligence claim of the parents once the full story of leaving their son, Anthony, in the company of his animal brothers was revealed.

Her testimony ended with the dramatic finding of the bodies of Roberto and Esther in what seemed like a murder/suicide and the conclusion that it was the same gun used to kill Pablo Jiménez and Pablo's parents.

Flickinger did very little on cross examination, smart enough to know it was about to get a whole lot worse. Court adjourned for the day with the admonition from the court that the jury was not to discuss the case with anyone, once again a warning that was worth just about the breath it took to say the words.

As they were packing up to leave, Flickinger, who had been talking to Annette Miller, came up to Will and said the carrier was willing to pay $100,000 to settle. Will looked at his adversary, looked at Miller in the back of the courtroom, and said to him, "James, you wouldn't take that for this case and you know we won't either."

Flickinger nodded. "See you tomorrow, Will."

Will got back to the office, confirmed that he had Dr. Janis Davenport, the national forensic expert on sexual abuse on children with disabilities, and Dr. David Dowling, the local psychiatrist who had examined Anthony, teed up and ready to go. Both assured them they were 'locked and loaded.'

He got back to the townhouse emotionally drained and was met at the door by Alex with a Jameson's neat in her hand which she gave him before he had even crossed the threshold. Half the glass was gone in one long sip.

"Thanks, babe."

He got out of his trial clothes and joined her in the hot tub with a second Jameson's.

"I saw your opening."

"And?"

A small smile. "Well, as they say, for an opening statement, it was a pretty good closing argument."

Will laughed for the first time in what seemed like weeks.

"I wondered how many times I could say 'negligence' before somebody would say something."

"No kidding, but James was between a rock and a hard place. Object and everybody remembers the word he objected to; don't object and everybody remembers the word because you used it more than any other word in the entire opening."

"And your point?"

He went on. "They offered us a $100,000 at the end of the day."

"Insurance woman?"

Will nodded.

"What did you say?"

“Told Flickinger he wouldn’t take that for this case and neither would I.”

“Gotta talk it over with Anthony and Jackie, don’t you?”

“I guess. In the morning.”

Chapter Thirty Four

Day Two

The next morning Will spoke with Jackie about the $100,000 offer. She had full authority to say yes or no on Anthony's behalf and $100,000 was more money, even with fees and costs, than Anthony had ever seen in his life. Plus with the home and the land now that he was the only heir at law, it might make a difference in his life. On the other hand, she knew what was coming today with the testimony of Dr. Davenport and Dr. Dowling and knew that no amount of money would ever make Anthony Jiménez whole.

"Tell Flickinger we'll take $490,000 of the $500,000 policy and promise we won't try to collect any overage over the $500,000 policy limits. But if they won't take that and if we get a verdict over the limits, we're coming after them big time for bad faith."

"Got it. Thanks, Jackie."

The first day after opening statements, Jackie and Anthony had left the courtroom and gone back to the office as Will had promised the jury. Today he was at home. Will saw no benefit whatsoever to him hearing from the experts.

When they got to the courtroom, Will relayed Jackie's message. He saw Flickinger go back behind the bar between the spectators and the lawyers and judge and speak briefly to Annette Miller. Will saw her shake her head and thought to himself 'game on.'

The first witness was Dr. David Dowling. In his 50's he had been a practicing psychiatrist for almost 30 years the first eight of which had been in the US Army working with veterans coming back from war with post-traumatic stress disorder. Since his discharge as a full Colonel, he had stayed in the Army Reserves in Albuquerque and had developed an interest in sexual abuse among children and, later, sexual abuse among children with disabilities. He had a private practice concentrating on children and adults who were victims of sexual abuse. There was no shortage of patients.

After having been qualified as an expert, he explained that Will Bennett had first called him about Anthony Jiménez and what he had been through. He agreed to take him on as a patient for free because of the horrors he had been through. Based on his experience and testing, he said that Anthony was on the autism spectrum from birth but that it was difficult to tell what his future would have looked like had he been raised in a normal, loving family given the level of abuse he went through.

In excruciating detail, he then went on to explain to the jury what Anthony told him had been done to him by mother, father and brothers. At one point in the testimony, a short recess needed to be taken because one of the jurors had gotten sick to her stomach.

Will then asked about the time period when Roberto and Esther Jiménez had moved from the house into their apartment leaving Anthony with his brothers.

"Dr. Dowling, based on your years of experience working with people who have been sexually and abused in the family setting for years on end, do you have an opinion more probable than not what was going through Anthony's parents' minds when they left their autistic son with his brothers?"

Flickinger. "Objection. Speculation. How can this witness possibly testify what was in the minds of his parents?"

153

Judge Peck. "Mr. Bennett?"

The trap had been set. "Let me lay some additional foundation, Your Honor."

"Dr. Dowling, how can you possibly testify what was in the minds of Anthony's parents when they left him with his brothers?"

"Throughout my career working with these families, time and again even with the horror of what the parents have done to their children, they still feel some love and some remorse and so they take steps to make amends…here removing themselves from the house where they had perpetrated their horror, they were hoping against hope that maybe the brothers would change. They were wrong, of course, but were doing the best they could with the horror they had created.

And one other thing, Mr. Bennett. The proof is in the pudding. When Roberto and Esther Jiménez realized what they had done, they took the only option left." He paused.

"They killed themselves."

Will let the silence overwhelm the courtroom for a moment.

"Doctor, what does the future hold for Anthony Jiménez?"

He paused again. "I think Anthony is one of the most remarkable people I have ever met. He has confronted these demons as well as he can and he has shown a resiliency that is remarkable. But…" And he turned to the jury. "…he will never, ever have a normal life given what was done to him."

Silence again. "Nothing further, Your Honor."

"Ladies and Gentlemen, we will take our morning break at this time. Again, please do not discuss the case among yourselves. Mr. Becerra, would you escort the jury to the jury room? We're adjourned."

"All rise."

On the way back into the courtroom, Will passed Flickinger and Miller in an animated conversation in the hallway. Miller was saying something gesturing in a way that left no doubt that she was unhappy about something.

Court reconvened and Dr. Dowling went back to the witness chair.

"Mr. Flickinger, any cross examination?"

"Yes, Your Honor." And James Flickinger rose to the lectern. "Dr. Dowling, I want to ask you about your conclusion that Anthony's parents felt really badly about leaving him with his sadistic, sick brothers. Their sons."

"All right."

"Do you really want this jury to believe that these monsters of parents felt remorse and sadness when they had done what all they had done and then had left Anthony to his brothers who were even worse than they were?"

"Yes, and may I explain why?"

The great conundrum for a trial lawyer. Say 'sure' and you get blasted by the explanation. Say 'no I'm asking the questions here' and you look like an asshole if the witness has any credibility at all.

Flickinger took the latter approach. "I'm asking the questions, Doctor, all you need to do is answer them."

Will saw one juror flinch and two others crossed their arms. Never a good sign. Dr. Dowling had credibility.

"So the parents go on their merry way, know they're leaving their son to be raped over and over again by his brothers, and it's OK for them to do that?"

Calmly. "Of course, it's not OK, Mr. Flickinger, and may I explain?"

James Flickinger had tried a lot of cases, he hated this one, and this cross exam, mandated by a directive from Annette Miller was not going well…at all.

"Again, I'm asking the questions, Doctor. And then you conclude that, because of remorse, they killed themselves?"

"Yes, in part."

"Nothing further."

"Redirect, Mr. Bennett?"

"Yes, Your Honor. I hesitate to say this, but just a few."

"That's what they all say, Mr. Bennett."

"I understand, Your Honor."

Will turned to the witness.

"Dr. Dowling, a few follow up questions that Mr. Flickinger wouldn't let you answer." Sometimes he couldn't just help himself. "Their lawyer describes his clients as 'monsters,' and yet you opine they would still feel remorse and sadness over what they did to their son. Please explain."

"From the time he was born, Anthony was different but it wasn't a difference you could see on an X-ray or a crutch that he had to use or a brace he had to wear because of a withered arm. He was different in a very different way. He didn't look like his brothers, he didn't act like them, and he didn't do the things that Mr. and Mrs. Jiménez saw in their other sons. Families go two ways. One, they love the so called 'different ones' as much, if not more, than the 'normal ones' or they go the other way, ashamed for whatever reason, cultural or otherwise, that there is something wrong with them because of what Anthony was. Not of his own doing and not of their own doing. Nevertheless, they're ashamed and do awful things because of it."

"And what about leaving their 'different' son to the sadistic brothers 'to be raped over and over again by his brothers' to use Mr. Flickinger's words?"

"Mr. Bennett, I don't condone any of this. I am simply telling you this is what happens in families that see a 'different child/young man' and don't take the time or don't have the education or the resources or the means to understand why somebody like Anthony is different. His condition is nobody's fault and nobody's to blame." His voice for the first time rose an octave or two. "But…" And he stopped.

"Finally, and I promise, Your Honor, why the murder/suicide?"

"Because somewhere along the way, whether it was faith or conscience or guilt, they finally understood and couldn't live with it."

"Thank you, Dr. Dowling, nothing further." The judge excused him.

"Next witness, Mr. Bennett?"

"Thank you, Your Honor, Plaintiff calls Dr. Janis Davenport."

Janis Davenport looked like she walked out of central casting as a physician. Tall, in good shape, carefully coiffed silver hair, and dressed impeccably in a gray suit and blue blouse. She spoke with a Boston accent having grown up there and having lived her whole life in the area.

Will walked Dr. Davenport through her credentials. Undergrad and medical school at Harvard, residency in psychiatry at Johns Hopkins in Baltimore, and two Fellowships at Harvard and Yale specializing in the diagnosis and treatment of autism.

"Dr. Davenport, would you explain to the ladies and gentlemen of the jury what autism is?"

The doctor smiled and turned to the jury. "In medical terms, autism is a neurodevelopmental disorder that is characterized by impaired social interaction, impaired verbal and non-verbal communication, and restricted and repetitive behavior. More simply, the brain develops differently than in most people and, as a result, the electrical impulses that drive most, and I use the word in quotes, 'normal' people are out of whack in people with autism."

"Are people born with it?"

"We think so. Most children, and it is far more prevalent in boys than girls, are diagnosed by the age of three. All of you have heard the word "spectrum" and the reason we use that term is that there is a wide range of individuals along the spectrum of autism. Some of the severe cases will never lead anywhere near a normal life and some have to be institutionalized; others at the other end of the spectrum are high functioning individuals who, with certain social impairments, can lead relatively normal lives."

"Anthony has some unusual physical characteristics. Is that common or uncommon in your experience?"

"It's certainly not uncommon because as the brain is developing abnormally, it can also create disturbances that manifest themselves in physical abnormalities."

"Part of the spectrum?"

"Yes."

"What about treatment for people on the spectrum?"

"We have come a very long way from the days when individuals were subject to electroshock therapy, lobotomies, mental institutions and the like and that is one of the reasons why I have spent my life studying autism…trying to figure out how best to treat it. These days the four categories of treatment fall into behavioral and communication therapy; medical and dietary therapy; occupational and physical therapy, and complementary therapy such as art or music therapy."

Dr. Davenport went on to explain each of the different therapies and the advantages each brings to the patient.

"Is there a cure for autism, Doctor?"

She paused for a long minute and finally shook her head. "While I would never say never, I think it's unlikely we will find a 'cure' at least in the near future. Instead, we concentrate on helping people with autism find better ways to live with the condition."

"Have you met Anthony Jiménez?"

"I have. I had the honor of spending yesterday afternoon with Anthony."

Bennett could feel Flickinger's head flip up out of the corner of his eye standing at the lectern. This was news to him.

"Before you met with him, what did you review?"

"I had the opportunity to review all of the medical records for Anthony and specifically the records of Dr. Dowling. In addition, I was here to hear Dr. Dowling's testimony this morning in court."

"Based on your review of Dr. Dowling's records, based on listening to his testimony, based on your years of experience working with patients on the spectrum, and based upon your exam of Anthony yesterday, have you come to an opinion, within a reasonable degree of psychiatric certainty, whether Anthony is a spectrum person?"

"I have."

"Would you tell the ladies and gentlemen of the jury what that opinion is?"

Janis Davenport turned and faced the jury.

"I wholeheartedly agree with Dr. Dowling that Anthony Jiménez is a remarkable man who has endured more than any human being should. He is certainly on the spectrum and his condition has been made far worse because of what was done to him. Had he been diagnosed at the earliest possible time, say, by the age of three, there were treatment modalities even twenty years ago that would have been of immense help. Unfortunately, his parents chose to hide him away rather than get the treatment he needed.

Because of that, Anthony will never be able to live without some sort of supervision, without some sort of societal structure.

And here's the worst part of all, ladies and gentlemen. Anthony Jiménez has tested out as a genius from all of his IQ testing. He is, to put it mildly, brilliant." All eyes were on Dr. Davenport as she continued.

"What makes this whole situation so troubling are two things. Anthony, by nature, is a gentle, good soul as are many people on the spectrum and while it is difficult for him sometimes to communicate with people, that doesn't mean he isn't loving and kind. He is. And secondly and even more awful, because he is so brilliant, he knew exactly what was happening to him."

Silence. Silence. Complete and utter silence.

Finally. "Thank you, Dr. Davenport. No further questions."

Flickinger: "I have no questions."

Judge Peck looked at the clock on the wall and announced the noon recess to reconvene at 1:30. The bailiff ushered the jury out and the judge left the bench.

Dr. Davenport stepped down from the witness stand.

Chapter Thirty Five

Anthony Takes the Stand

Will thanked the doctor profusely and promised he would call as soon as the trial was over. Liz LaRue gathered the doctor up to get her to the airport to get her home.

Will walked back to the office to meet Jackie and Anthony who were waiting for him in one of the conference rooms. Anthony was to be the last witness and Jackie and Will had thought long and hard on how best to get him up and down from the witness stand as quickly as possible. Will was pleasantly surprised to find Anthony clean, shaved, and dressed in a handsome polo shirt and new Dockers. He seemed amazingly calm especially with his hand firmly clasped in Jackie's. They ate deli sandwiches and Will told Anthony about how the trial was going and, in a very abbreviated and censored fashion, what Doctor Dowling and Dr. Davenport had talked about.

One of the crucial issues continued to be to prove to the jury that Anthony's parents had been negligent in leaving him with his brothers. It was the only way to trigger the insurance coverage that Annette Miller was so jealously guarding and Will so wanted to get to especially now that he had made a demand within the policy limits. If they could convince the jury that the parents were negligent and if they could get a verdict in excess of the policy limits of $500,000, then they might have a chance of proving that the insurance company had been in 'bad faith' by not settling and then have the opportunity to go after the insurance company for anything over the limits.

It was complicated, there were lots of 'Ifs', and it was a long shot, but well worth going after.

Shortly after 1:00, Jackie, Will and Anthony walked over to the courtroom and settled into their seats at counsel table. Will continued to be awestruck by Anthony's calm as he sat quietly between Will and Jackie, his hand still in Jackie's.

James Flickinger and Peter Flemming walked in and sat across the way. At precisely 1:30, the bailiff came out, asked if counsel were ready, and went to get the jury. As each of the eight walked into the courtroom, their eyes fixed on Anthony. They took their seats eyes still glued to the Plaintiff's table.

"All rise."

Judge Peck entered from his chambers, took his seat, and nodded that the rest of the courtroom could be seated as well.

"Mr. Bennett, your next witness."

"Your Honor, the Plaintiff calls Anthony Jiménez with a special request."

The judge raised an eyebrow.

"We would ask that his Guardian, Jackie Lapointe, be allowed to sit next to him during his testimony. She has become a very important part of Mr. Jiménez's life and is a great emotional support."

Flickinger knew Will had sprung a trap and, in some small way, admired him for it. Properly, the issue should have been taken up outside the presence of the jury but Flickinger knew he was, once again, between a rock and a hard place. He'd been there before with the cross of Dr. Dowling and wasn't going to make the same mistake.

"Certainly no objection, Your Honor."

Manny Becerra moved a second chair into the witness area and Jackie and Anthony seated themselves next to each other hand in hand.

"Would you introduce yourself to the jury?"

"Anthony Jiménez."

"How old are you, Anthony?"

"24. I think."

"Do you know when your birthday is?"

"No."

"Why not?"

"Nobody ever told me."

"Who is Dr. David Dowling, Anthony?"

"He's a doctor I see who tries to help me."

"What does he help you with?"

"All of the things that have happened to me."

"Does it help to talk to him?"

"Yes. Some."

"Anthony, Dr. Dowling talked to the jury this morning and talked about some of the things you've been through. When you talk to him, do you tell him the truth?"

"Yes."

"Why?"

"Because I know the only way I'll get better is to tell the truth about what happened to me."

"What you have told him. Is it all true?"

James Flickinger was half way out of his chair to object. Anthony had not been there for his testimony so there was no way he could know what he had testified to. He thought better of it and sat back down. He had enough enemies in the jury box without making it worse.

"Yes."

"Anthony, I want to talk to you about the time you were living with your parents in an apartment and they took you back to the house on Desert Drive. Do you remember that?"

"Yes."

"Tell us what happened?"

"They kept me in a room by myself for a long time. Then one day, I think it was during the day, my mom came in and she was crying. My daddy had been in a little while before that and he had hurt me like he had before. Mommy had watched. She told me she couldn't stand what they were doing to me in the apartment any more and she said the only safe place was with my brothers. Otherwise, my daddy would just keep doing what he did."

"Did you say anything?"

"No."

"Why not? Weren't you afraid of your brothers just as much as your dad?"

For just a moment, Will thought he had gone too far. He saw tears in Anthony's eyes and could see Jackie tighten her grip on his hand.

"Yes, Will, but I knew mom loved me and she was trying to get me away from daddy. It was the only place she could think I'd be safe."

"And were you safe?"

"No."

"Did you ever see your parents again?"

Will could swear he saw a shadow cross over Anthony's eyes and wondered what that was all about.

"No."

"As far as you know, did your parents know what your brothers were doing to you?"

"No."

"I have no further questions. Thank you, Anthony. Mr. Flickinger may have some questions for you."

Judge Peck looked over at the jury and noted at least half of them were in tears. He called for a fifteen minute recess and promptly left the bench. The jury was ushered out by the bailiff.

There was a hush over the courtroom as Jackie led Anthony off the stand and out into the hallway to go to the bathroom. Will sat at counsel table as emotionally drained as he had ever felt in his life. A moment later, he felt a presence at his side. It was Flickinger.

"Miller's willing to go to $250,000, Will."

Will Bennett took a deep breath.

"James, you're a good lawyer and I respect you. You're in a terrible position and I get it. I've been there. But no amount of money is going to make a difference to this young man and he has now been through so much in this lawsuit that he needs to at least have a jury tell him they understand what he's been through. The chance for this insurance company to have done right is long gone. I'll talk to Jackie and Anthony but I know what the answer is."

Flickinger nodded and walked away.

When court started up again and before Anthony and Jackie could get back to the witness stand, James Flickinger stood up.

"I have no questions of Mr. Jiménez, Your Honor."

"Thank you, Mr. Flickinger. Mr. Bennett?"

"Plaintiff rests his case, Your Honor."

Flickinger stood again and told the court he had two motions he wanted to bring.

Judge Peck thought for a moment and decided that by the time the motions were argued and he had ruled, it would be too late in the day to get anything else accomplished so he excused the jury with the usual warnings not to talk about the case and to be back in court the next morning at 8:30. There was a palpable sense of relief on the jurors' faces. They needed a break.

After the jury was gone, Jackie and Anthony also left.

Once they were gone, Judge Peck asked Mr. Flickinger to proceed.

"Your Honor, the first motion is to exclude any consideration by the jury for events that occurred before four years ago because of the statute of limitations against all of the defendants."

Will knew this was coming. New Mexico law says that you have to bring a case for assault within four years of the actual assault or it's barred by what's called the statute of limitations. God knows what had happened in the last four years was plenty to get a strong verdict although Will argued first that, given Anthony's disabilities, there should be no limitations period whatsoever and, second, given that he was a virtual prisoner of his family all of his life, there was no way he could get the legal help he needed.

"Counsel, given the testimony of Dr. Dowling, Dr. Davenport, and the Plaintiff himself, I don't think his disabilities are an obstacle whatsoever. However, I agree with Mr. Bennett that because he was a virtual prisoner all of his life, he did not have the opportunity to seek legal recourse at any time in his life until he was freed and found Mr. Bennett. At this point in the trial and before hearing your case, Mr. Flickinger, I'll deny the motion. You mentioned a second motion."

"Yes, Your Honor. The Defendants move that, as a matter of law, the negligence count against Mr. and Mrs. Jiménez should be dismissed. As abhorrent as these acts are, there is nothing to suggest that the parents were negligent. They were animals, they were sadistic, they were human scum. Nothing they did was negligent, it was all intentional."

"Well, Mr. Flickinger, I can hardly wait for your closing argument extolling the virtues of the rest of the Jiménez family. Mr. Bennett, your response."

Will had known with absolute certainty this one was coming. Annette Miller, in the back of the courtroom, had been waiting for this one. If the judge granted the motion, there was no insurance coverage and she was a hero. If the judge denied the motion and let it go to the jury and if the jury found negligence on the part of the parents, she'd be dusting off her resume.

"The issue of negligence centers around the decision of the parents to take Anthony back to the Desert Drive home and leave him with his brothers. Dr. Dowling testified that they did it out of guilt and remorse and thought he would be safer there. Anthony testified about his mother coming to him and wanting him to be away from "daddy" so he couldn't hurt him anymore. It was a conscious decision and they got it wrong. That is negligence: duty to their son to keep him safe, breach of that duty to put him in harm's way, causation, and damages. That's a jury question."

Judge Peck asked for a fifteen minute recess and left the bench.

Fifteen minutes stretched into forty-five minutes and finally the court was back in session.

"I have carefully considered Defendants' motion on the negligence issue. In all of the years as a judge, I've never been confronted with an issue where the conduct was so egregious and so horrific, that it eliminated a theory of negligence. We all know what this motion is about and we all know why Mr. Bennett presented the case he did and why Mr. Flickinger cross examined Dr. Dowling the way he did. It's not, as my daughter would say, 'rocket surgery.' I don't think I'm in a position to take away the decision from the jury at this point. Rather, I'd like to hear the rest of the trial, have the jury deliberate, and then make a decision. I'm taking the motion under advisement.

Mr. Flickinger, tell us about your case and who you intend to call."

Flickinger looked back at Miller who shook her head.

"The defense rests, Your Honor."

"All right. Let's take a half hour for me to deal with a couple of other matters and then get together in my chambers to talk jury instructions. We're in recess."

Chapter Thirty Six

Haggling

One of the little-known secrets about the practice of law is what happens in the judge's chambers away from the jury and away from the spectators. Arguing over jury instructions, that is, what the judge is going to tell the jury is the law and their duty to follow it, is like making sausage. It may look good when it's in open court but getting there is messy.

Judge Peck called Will and James into his chambers toward the end of the day.

"All right, gents. What do we have to decide? Will, you're the Plaintiff. You go first."

"Judge, most of the instructions are pretty basic and I think we can agree on almost everything with the standard instructions in the New Mexico jury instructions. Where James and I are going to hang up is that I want an instruction to the jury that they may consider whether it was negligence on the part of the parents to give their son over to his brothers and I want a box on the verdict form that asks: 'Were Roberto and/or Esther Jiménez negligent in turning over Anthony Jiménez to his brothers at the Desert Drive home roughly 2 ½ years ago?' It's no secret why I want it. There's half a million dollars in home owner's insurance with MISMO, I've made a demand within policy limits that's been rejected, and if there's a verdict over the policy limits, I want to preserve a 'bad faith' case against MISMO."

"James, your thoughts?"

There was a pause that lasted far longer than either the judge or Will thought was necessary. Will looked over and was stunned to see tears in his opponent's eyes. He was truly struggling for words.

Finally and with a voice that shook with emotion. "Judge, I'm a dad. I have two daughters and a son. My son has Asperger's which is a form of autism. He's doing well but struggles with all of the issues that both Dowling and Davenport talked about. To think that because he's a little different, he should be subjected to what Anthony went through is one of the most abhorrent things I've seen in my lifetime.

I hate this case more than anything in my life. I want to do the right thing and the right thing for my clients, the estates of the mom and dad and Anthony's brothers, and the right thing is to trigger the insurance. In open court I will argue that the requested instruction and box on the verdict form is against the great weight of the evidence, against all of the testimony, and fraught with enough error to guarantee an appeal of any over limits verdict. Within the confines of this chamber and with the understanding that what I just said is confidential, give the damn instruction, put the box on the verdict form, and leave it up to the jury."

Now it was Will's turn and the judge's turn to tear up.

Judge Peck took a deep breath. "Thank you, gentlemen. You agree on the rest of the instructions so let's go back into court and put the objections on the record." He paused. "You both should know I am extremely proud of the way you have tried this case but, far more importantly, proud of being a member of our profession because it includes people like yourselves. Thank you for allowing me to be a part of this. And that's absolutely confidential."

They went back into the courtroom, Will made his motion to include negligence both in the jury instruction and on the verdict form and James Flickinger made an impassioned argument against it for all of the reasons he had cited in chambers.

Judge Peck asked for a short recess to consider the arguments and returned a few minutes later.

"This is a very close call and I appreciate Mr. Flickinger's arguments. However, with the directed verdict on this issue still under advisement and with the testimony as it exists, I will allow the instruction on negligence and the question on the verdict form. Mr. Bennett, if you will prepare a proposed verdict form for review ahead of closing arguments in the morning?"

"I will, Your Honor."

"Thank you. We're in recess and I'll see you in chambers tomorrow at 8:00 to go over anything before closing arguments. We're adjourned."

Chapter Thirty Seven

Showtime

When he got back to the office, Jackie and Will met to talk about the effect of Anthony's testimony on him. Will had thought he had been a rock star but Jackie said it had devastated him to talk even with the testimony as short as it was. That's all Will needed.

"Then he's not coming to the closing arguments. Get him home and tell him we'll call him when we get a verdict."

"Good call, Chief. Thanks."

Will went out to the waiting room where Anthony was sitting.

"You OK?"

"No matter how it turns out, Will, thank you. I'm glad the story got told."

"We'll call as soon as we know something, Anthony. You were amazing today. Thanks for your courage."

Anthony stood up and hugged his lawyer. And Jackie came out to take him home.

Will went back to the office and sat down to work on the verdict form. It was a series of questions that the jury was to answer in their deliberations. Most of them were easy.

'Did the Defendants sexually abuse the plaintiff over many years?' ____Yes or No.'

'Was the Plaintiff harmed by the sexual abuse?' ____ Yes or No.'

'Did the Plaintiff suffer damages as a result of the sexual abuse?' _____ Yes or No.'

'If you answered 'Yes' that the Plaintiff suffered damages, what is the dollar amount of damages he suffered up to the date of your verdict?' $_____.'

'If the Plaintiff will suffer damages into the future for the rest of his life, what is the amount of those damages?' $_____.'

'Did the Defendants act intentionally?' _____ Yes or No.'

'If you find the Defendants acted intentionally, are they responsible for punitive damages? If you answer the question 'Yes,' what is the total of the punitive damages they are responsible for?' $_____.'

'Were Roberto and/or Esther Jiménez negligent, as I have defined that term, in returning the Plaintiff to the Desert Drive home approximately 2 ½ years ago?' _____ Yes or No.'

'If your answer is 'Yes' to the question, what are the damages the Plaintiff suffered up to the date of your verdict?' $_____.'

'If your answer is 'Yes' to the question, if the Plaintiff will suffer damages into the future for the rest of his life, what is the amount of those damages.' $_____.'

Liz LaRue took the form to drop off at the office supply store down the street to get it blown up on to a large foam board and then went home to be back to pick it up in the morning when they opened at 8:00 AM. That was that.

Will sat in the stillness of the office and thought about the closing argument.

Trial lawyers in trial lawyer classes say that they prepare the closing argument first because it helps them focus on the conclusions they want the jury to come to and then they back it out to what they need the witnesses to say to get there. Will had been a trial lawyer for a long time and he had never met another trial lawyer in his or her career who actually did that. A good idea but just not one anybody ever did.

Nevertheless, Will did keep a folder that was called simply 'notes' and whenever something would come to him, he would jot it down and put it in the file to look at if he needed it. One failing of his system was that some of his best ideas came after a couple of Jameson's Irish and sometimes the writing was damn near indecipherable…and he had good hand writing. He pulled it out and looked through what he had written. From the very first piece of paper in the file when the firm agreed to represent Anthony Jiménez, 'Lost and Alone' had been the theme that had driven the litigation and it was how he had started his opening statement. It still resonated, it still felt right and true, and that made the rest easy. He made sure that he was incorporating the jury instructions into the argument that the jury would hear from the judge and he especially made sure the verdict form would be ready for him to make the check marks for the jury to follow.

Will decided not to spend a lot of time on the horror. Even in a short trial like this one, the jury was clearly emotionally exhausted. Going over in closing what they had heard from the doctors and from Anthony seemed to be overkill. They didn't need that. The jury clearly got the case.

He thought about his 'sit down' and 'the ask.' Both how to end with the drama of the moment and how to ask for damages. It was always the most difficult because, unless you had read the jury right, you could either ask for too much or too little. Will thought about it and came to a decision that, in his gut, felt right.

Will picked up his notes, the 'notes' file, turned off the lights and felt an overwhelming urge to be back in Alex's space.

On the drive home, he considered the price that trial lawyers paid. Will loved being in the courtroom and loved the adrenaline rush. What he had come to hate was everything that went with it…the overwhelming crush that the case took over in his life. You ate it, you slept it (or didn't), it hurt your relationships, it was all consuming. Some were able to compartmentalize better than others. When he was a defense lawyer, it was easier; it was about money. But as a plaintiff's attorney, you were carrying somebody's life on your back. Harder, much harder.

Alex greeted Will at the door with a Jameson's in one hand, a plate with some cheese and crackers in the other, and dressed in a loosely tied bathrobe.

"Get your clothes off, boyfriend, and join me in the hot tub. You got some 'splaining to do."

It took him all of three minutes and he was in the tub. He went through the day, summarized the testimony of Dowling and Davenport and Anthony, and then talked about the conversation in Judge Peck's chambers and Flickinger's disclosure about his son. He talked about his closing argument and how it was structured.

"Jesus, Alex, I've been talking and talking and talking. You still awake?"

She laughed that Alex laugh. "I remember you talking about Davenport. Was there something after that?"

He splashed her and laughed with her. He was on the last lap and already feeling the relief that comes when it's over.

"Bring it home, Will."

That night he slept as well as he had in weeks. 'Bring it home.'

And the next morning, that's exactly what he did.

"Lost and alone, ladies and gentlemen. That has been Anthony Jiménez's life, his whole twenty four years of life, and why? Because he was different. He looked different, he acted different, and he was different. And so it was that for the better part of his life, he was tortured and tormented and assaulted by his father and his brothers while his mother let it happen. You have heard enough of the details that I don't need to talk about them because what you have already heard is enough to haunt you for weeks and months to come. You don't need to hear it again from me.

2 ½ years ago, something changed with Roberto or maybe just Esther Jiménez. Whether it was guilt or remorse or a combination we'll never know but what we do know was that the decision was made to get Anthony out of the apartment and away from his father. The only place, because it was the only place Anthony knew, was to go back to the home on Desert Drive. To his parents there was no other option.

Judge Peck is going to instruct you on the law of negligence and one of the things you will be asked to decide is whether Anthony's parents were negligent in returning him to a place where the horror would continue. He will tell you there are four elements to negligence: one, a duty and there clearly was one here because they were his parents…what greater duty is there…and they had the duty to get him out of harm's way; two, a breach of that duty and that is clearly here because they put him in a place where he spent 2 ½ years living in a garden shed; three, causation and that goes without saying; and four, damages and how can anybody argue that Anthony Jiménez wasn't damaged in those weeks and months imprisoned in a garden shed."

Will pointed to the blowup of the verdict form that was on an easel in front of the jury.

"When you get to this question: Were Roberto and/or Esther Jiménez negligent…?" Will took a big red marker and wrote 'Yes' on the line. "The answer must be 'Yes.'"

Will went through the rest of the verdict form and, very quickly, pointed out why all of the questions needed to be answered 'Yes.'

He ended with this. "I haven't filled in the lines about damages and what amount seems right because, honestly, I don't know what to say. If Anthony had all of the money in the world, he would pay it in a heartbeat not to have been given the life he has been forced to lead. If you choose to give him one dollar – one dollar – for all that he's been through, then so be it. No amount of money can compensate for the harm that's been done and what he will live with for the rest of his life. But let me say this. If your verdict sends a message to those families here in Albuquerque, or maybe even to a larger audience, who regularly abuse or beat or sexually assault their children or their spouses, that six men and women, strangers just three days ago, who have become witnesses to the unspeakable harm such abuse causes, say with your verdict 'Enough. No more,' then justice will have been served."

Will Bennett looked each of them in the eye, stood at the lectern for a quiet few seconds, and then returned to counsel table. He had spoken for 13 minutes.

"Mr. Flickinger?"

"Thank you, Your Honor, and thank you, ladies and gentlemen, for your attention over these past days. Mr. Bennett is a very good lawyer and I have great respect for him but he is wrong in a couple of respects. First of all, this isn't about negligence of the parents in taking Anthony Jiménez back to his brothers. That wasn't negligence, it was an intentional act that only continued the unspeakable torture of Anthony. The answer to that question on the verdict form must be 'No.'"

Flickinger stopped for a moment to look at his notes before continuing on and, in that moment gathering himself, he remembered for the first time that one of the members of the jury was an insurance adjuster. He had left him on the jury figuring he would bring reason to the rest of the jury to avoid a runaway verdict and, secondly and more practically, he had run out of challenges. What he hadn't figured on was that Judge Peck would give a negligence instruction and that the adjuster would know exactly what the answer to that question would mean if there were insurance coverage. Flickinger looked up briefly at the adjuster who, with his arms crossed, was having none of it. 'Ruh roh.'

But, to his great credit, he soldiered on for a few more moments and then at the end suggested that a proper verdict to compensate Anthony for what he had been through was $100,000.

There are two schools of thought about whether the defense should offer what it thinks the case is worth. The first is that if there is a good defense to the case, then why do it? The other school of thought is that if the defense doesn't give a number, the only number the jury hears is the Plaintiff's. Here, where there really is no defense on liability, the question is 'what number.' Too low and you get pummeled. Too high and it becomes a floor for a higher verdict.

As he was going to see in a few hours, Flickinger picked 'too low.'

Rebuttal was short and brutal.

"$100,000. $100,000 for unimaginable pain and horror that lasted for almost Anthony's entire life time? Simply because he was different? Like he had a choice? Ladies and gentlemen, $100,000 is a joke, an insult. $1,000,000 would be a joke and an insult. Ten times that can't undo the harm. This is about justice, pure and simple. Justice. Your verdict won't give Anthony Jiménez peace and it won't bring him happiness. That will never happen. But your verdict will give him justice. That's what he deserves." He sat down.

Judge Peck instructed the jury on the law, made sure they had a copy of the verdict form to fill out, and excused the two alternate jurors from further duty. He had Mr. Becerra take them to the jury room to deliberate. It was 10:00 AM. Day three.

James Flickinger and Will Bennett shook hands and both left the courthouse for their offices. Deep in thought, Will wondered whether there was anything else he could have done but decided he had given it the best shot he could. He knew the jury would return a verdict in Anthony's favor but how much and how it would be collected were the bigger questions.

Jackie and Anthony were in one of the conference rooms when he got back and they again ordered sandwiches to be brought in. Will explained to the both of them what had happened in the closing arguments and they talked quietly about the trial and some of the obstacles that lay ahead. Will thought to himself that Anthony had never looked better. He had put on some weight and the color in his face was far healthier than it had been those many months before when he had shown up unannounced at the offices of Johnston & Blackwell. What a journey it had been.

At 3:20 Will's cell phone rang. It was Manny Becerra, the bailiff.

"Will, they have a verdict."

Will hung up, stood up, and got his briefcase. Anthony stood as well.

"I'd like to be there, Will, if you think it would be all right."

Will looked at Jackie who nodded 'yes.'

"OK then. Let's the three of us go see what they did."

Flickinger and Peter Flemming, the Personal Representative of the four estates, were already at counsel table.

Jackie, Will, and Anthony set up at their table closest to the jury box.

"All rise." Judge Peck entered the courtroom.

"Please be seated. Is there anything we need to discuss before we bring the jury in?"

"No, Your Honor." Again in unison.

"Bailiff, would you get the jury please?"

The six members of the jury filed in and as they took their seats, all of them looked directly at Anthony.

“Would the foreperson please rise?”

The insurance adjuster stood up with the verdict form in his hand.

“Have you reached a verdict?”

“We have, Your Honor.”

“Please read the questions from the verdict form and your answers to the questions.”

The foreperson cleared his throat, put on his reading glasses, and began.

Chapter Thirty Eight

Aftermath

When Will and Jackie and Anthony got back to the office, they went into the conference room. All three were somber and quiet. Will stepped out for a minute to tell Liz about the verdict.

Her only comment. "Wow."

He went back in and said to the two of them.

"Well, what do you think?"

"Better than a sharp stick in the eye if I may say so."

"Anthony?"

Through free-flowing tears, the young man managed a smile.

"I'm just glad it's over, Will. Thank you so much for everything you all have done for me." More tears.

The jury had come back with $15 million dollars in compensatory damages for what had been done to Anthony and another $15 million dollars in punitive damages to do exactly what punitive damages are meant to do: Punish. Even with all of them dead, the jury wanted to make a statement that this was just evil. Talk about sending a message.

Just as importantly, the jury had answered 'Yes' to the question about whether Roberto and/or Esther Jiménez had been negligent. That answer not only triggered the insurance coverage that Annette Miller had been so jealously guarding but, far more importantly, set up a potential 'bad faith' claim against MISMO for not settling within policy limits. And in New Mexico, unlike a lot of states, insurance companies could be responsible not only for compensatory damages but also 'punies.' The potential, and it was only a potential at this point, was that MISMO could be on the hook for the full $30 million dollars.

Ms. Miller had left the courtroom as soon as the jury had answered the question of negligence.

Will explained to Anthony that there were plenty of hoops to jump through like post trial motions and appeals but that, on this given day, justice had been done.

"Jackie, would you take me home now?" More sadness in his voice and in his eyes. Will wondered why. A $30 million dollar verdict usually cheers people up.

"Sure, Anthony."

Anthony hugged Will goodbye and left with Jackie. And not a moment too soon. They just missed a gaggle of reporters and TV crews invading the Johnston & Blackwell lobby. To Will's knowledge, there had not been a single reporter covering the trial but news travels fast with this kind of verdict.

For the next half hour, Will answered questions about what had happened to Anthony over the years and his hope that the verdict would help at least ease the pain that, for sure, would never, could never, go away.

The last person to pack up to leave was Megan Dixon, the *Albuquerque Journal* reporter who had been friends with both Will and Alex for a long time. Will had given her the scoop in the Ruiz trial and she had never forgotten the favor.

"Will, if the verdict holds, can you collect anything?"

"Off the record for now?"

"Sure…as long as you tell me first." With a smile.

"But of course. It's a big problem and the short answer is 'I'm not sure.' There's the house and the property which is worth a chunk of change and will go to him as the closest living heir. There are a couple of life insurance policies in play except only his two brothers were named as contingent beneficiaries so we're in suit on that. And there was a home owner's policy that may be in play. But how it all shakes out will take time. Plus there will be the inevitable post-trial motions for a new trial or a request to have the judge lower the verdict or an appeal probably on the issue of instructing the jury on the negligence theory of the parents which when the jury answered 'Yes' triggered the insurance. Lots of moving parts, Megan."

"What happens to Anthony?"

Will shook his head. "I don't know." He paused for a long time. "We've applied for Social Security Disability and I would think he would get that for sure if the verdict doesn't hold. But what he does with his life is anybody's guess. Jackie LaPointe has been a godsend for him and has gotten him some lessons on reading and writing. He is a genius from the testing that they've done so maybe he gets an education and can do something with it.

The problem is that the damage done to a human being by those who are supposed to love him is permanent and can never change. How much of that he overcomes remains to be seen."

She closed her steno pad. "Any chance of doing a follow up story on him personally?"

"Boy, I don't know, Megan. If he's willing, you would be the one."

"Thanks, Will." Now her turn to pause. "A lot of lawyers wouldn't have taken this on, especially with no idea if there's a pot at the end of the rainbow. So, congratulations not on the verdict as much as having the guts to take the case in the first place."

He teared up, gave her a hug, and headed back to his office. Except that he was waylaid by every member of the firm, save Jackie, who dragged him into the conference room where champagne and chips and pretzels and dip awaited him.

Liz. "Little light on quality at this time of day and with this short of notice but we did the best we could. And somebody stopped by on her way home from work 'cause she heard there was a party going on and you know what a party animal she is."

A group at the end of the table parted and there was the Honorable herself, Alexandra Kennedy. She hugged him as hard as she could and this time, he couldn't stop the dam from overflowing with tears.

"You've always said 'winnin's better than losin'.' But this does seem a bit extreme even by your standards, Buckaroo."

They spent the next hour drinking champagne and eating chips and dip, one of Will's favorites of all time, and talking with the men and women who made up Johnston & Blackwell, all of whom Will counted among his best of friends.

At one point, he talked with Rosalind McManus, along with Jackie, the rock stars who were the future of the firm. "You and Jackie gonna let Anthony keep this money, Rosalind?"

"We sure as hell are. Judge Peck will not grant a new trial and he will not lower the damages. The big issue is the 'negligence' instruction and whether that holds up on appeal. My best guess is that they will file a notice of appeal on that issue and you'll get a phone call from Annette Miller's boss. I'm also guessing Ms. Miller is already no longer a Senior Claims Adjuster for MISMO Property and Casualty."

Will thought of Mark Nelson, the National Claims Manager for MISMO, and the guy that both Flickinger and Will had done work for. He thought Rosalind was right on both counts.

Will and Alex left the firm and drove home separately. They had both been careful not to over-indulge on the champagne on Will's part because he was exhausted and on Alex's part because having the Chief Judge stopped for impaired driving were very bad optics.

They made it home and promptly opened a new bottle of Tullamore Dew, a step up from their usual Irish whiskey, Jameson's. They went out on the patio and settled in.

"Jesus, Will, I think this is the biggest verdict in Bernalillo County history. There was that $27,000,000 verdict a few years ago against the power company for stray voltage hurting all those cows but that got reversed on appeal and ultimately settled. This and the Ruiz verdict are sort of putting you on the map about the same time you should be thinking of slowing down."

He thought about that comment. Will was in his late 50s and starting to feel it. He still loved the courtroom and the adrenaline rush but getting there was awful. But two of the best young lawyers he had ever met, Jackie LaPointe and Rosalind McManus, were every day taking on more and more responsibility for getting the cases ready and maybe there could be a role for him as the 11th hour lawyer, coming in at the last minute to actually try the case knowing that the young people had gotten it to where it had to be. It had worked in Ruiz and he wondered about that model.

He posed the question to Alex.

"Yeah, maybe. I've had both Rosalind and Jackie in court and they truly are spectacular. Rest of the judges feel the same way. So yeah, maybe." She picked up the bottle and poured another drink for both of them.

That night he was lying in bed and, as tired as he was, sleep wouldn't come. He kept thinking about Anthony Jiménez and everything he'd been through. Had they put him through even more agony just to get a verdict he might never see? The sadness in the young man's eyes haunted Will. He had listened to the experts and he had understood what they were saying. But unless you've walked in the shoes of a sexually abused person on top of being on the spectrum of autism on top of being a Mensa candidate by virtue of your IQ, how could you ever know?

Exhaustion, and a third Tullamore Dew, got the best of him, he spooned Alex and went to sleep.

The next morning, Alex got up at the usual time but let Will sleep blissfully on. She hoped he wasn't supposed to be some place important but knew that he had written off the whole week for the trial.

The *Journal* was on the front porch and the 'above the fold' article on page one was the verdict. The largest in the history of the state. And it ended by Megan Dixon saying the verdict was 'well deserved.' A picture of Will in the lobby of the law firm.

'Geez, he looks tired.'

She did something she almost never did. She made him breakfast, took it upstairs, woke him up, and gave him the paper. "You're famous. Today. Tomorrow we're back to normal. Except you left the toilet seat up again in the middle of the night.

So maybe famous until, say, noon. I love you, Will. Congrats again." And off to the shower.

While she was in the shower, Will looked over the tray she had brought up. It had been done with love and he knew that and he loved her more than he thought he could ever love anybody other than his daughter, Grace.

That having been said, Will had recognized early on in his relationship with Alex that cooking was not one of her strong suits. This breakfast was no exception. As near as he could put it together, her concept of scrambled eggs was to put some eggs in a frying pan, break the yokes, and then yell 'scrambled eggs' and magically they would turn out. So they were done really well on the frying pan side and soupy on the top. Toast was another challenge. He wasn't sure how, with a toaster in the kitchen, she could burn one side to black and have the other side untouched. But she had. And the coffee. It's not that easy to mess up a Keurig cup of coffee and they had been over it several times. Looking at the cup on the tray, the only thing he could think is that Alex was under the impression that one could use the cups several times over which in this case resulted in a very diluted cup that could well have been mistaken for a very bad urine specimen. Will had two options. Eat the food or run downstairs and dump it in the garbage disposal and head to Garcia's for a breakfast burrito with extra onions and green chili. He chose to do both. He ate what was edible, got downstairs and got rid of the rest while Alex was getting dressed, saw her off with a hug and a kiss and a thank you for breakfast, and then went straight to Garcia's. For breakfast and coffee. Perfect.

Will checked his email while he was waiting for his burrito. Lots of congratulations from colleagues in the area but the best one was from Margaret Espinoza and J.D. Rawlings: 'congrats on

justice being done. Save Friday afternoon, May 15. We've asked
our favorite judge to marry us in her chambers and we would love
to have you there. Margaret and J.D.'

        While he was at Garcia's, he read the article by Megan, felt
it was, in most respects, accurate and objective. 'Of course, he
would,' he thought to himself. 'It was a $30 million dollar verdict.'
He wondered vaguely how James Flickinger was feeling the day
after getting hit for $30 million. He shouldn't have worried.
Flickinger had gone through the same angst that Will had gone
through in terms of what he could have done differently. He had
been offered no options by MISMO and Annette Miller. If she had
pitched the limits or close to them, he could have gotten the case
settled short of trial and short of a $30 million dollar verdict. She
had chosen to roll the dice and had lost. Badly. James was pretty
sure this would be the last case he would see from MISMO. But
he would be mistaken.

Chapter Thirty Nine

The Wheels of Justice Turn Ever So Slowly

Two weeks after the verdict, the judgment got entered. With interest and costs, the total amount of the judgment was $30,450,000 dollars. A couple of days after that, Will got a call from James Flickinger to tell him that Emmett Myer of Myer and Associates would be handling the post-trial activity. Will was not surprised. Emmett specialized in appeals and had been handling the Ruiz appeal when it had settled. Will liked Emmett, respected him, and, if it had to be anybody, was glad it was him.

Silence. And then James said, "Will, I give you all the credit in the world for bringing the case in. Not sure you win on the insurance issue, but if I had to lose like this to somebody, I'd just as soon it was you."

"James, you were in an absolutely impossible situation from the day MISMO retained you. You handled it with courage and grace and great skill. And you're right, it may all get taken away but Anthony got to tell his story and that's huge."

"Agreed. Incidentally and I'd have to kill you if you repeated this but you may get a call from Mark Nelson. I'm guessing if there are settlement talks, it will come from Mark instead of Emmett. Put in a good word for me."

Will laughed. "Of course, James, take care of yourself."

"You too, Will. Bye."

"Bye."

A day later, Will got an email from Emmett Meyer, 'appreciate your attempts to keep me gainfully employed but couldn't you just get a verdict for a little less than $30 mil? We'll be filing the usual post trial 'God, Judge, how could you have gotten it so wrong' motions and assuming they go down in flames, we'll file the appeal. You and I both know our respective soft spots. We'll see what happens. E.'

Will replied, 'Always a pleasure, Emmett. Look forward to the first salvo.'

Chapter Forty

Love

Friday, May 15, dawned chilly and rainy, an anomaly in New Mexico that some in the state took personally, including the Chief Judge, Alexandra Kennedy.

"Of all the days it had to be cloudy, it had to be this one."

Will checked the radar. "The cavalry is on the way. Supposed to clear by about 11 and the service is at noon, right?"

"Don't know why I'm so nervous today. Just another wedding."

"No, Alex, it's not. This is a remarkable day for two remarkable people we care very much about. You should be nervous. Just try not to fuck it up."

She punched him in the shoulder just a little harder than a love tap.

"You always say just the right thing, counselor."

"It will go splendidly, my love."

She flipped him the bird on the way out the door.

At 11:45, Will cleared security at the courthouse and went up to Judge Kennedy's chambers. Karen Stillson, Judge Kennedy's case manager and best friend, greeted him at the door with a big hug.

"You never call, you never write, you never send me flowers…Good to see you, Will. Been a while."

"Must be your fault, Karen, can't be mine. Life OK?"

"Never better. And the two of you?"

"Never better. Unless you know something I don't."

"Oh sure, Will, and like I'd tell you if I did."

Karen had been a part of a very difficult chapter in the lives of Alex and Will and, like most of their friends, had been both amazed they had been able to put the band back together and overjoyed they had.

"She's in her office practicing."

He knocked and got the OK to come in. He had somehow missed how beautiful she was that morning before she left but she almost took his breath away. She had dressed in a beautiful white floor length dress, done just the right make up to make her eyes sparkle, and wore just enough jewelry to set off the white dress.

"Oh my God, Alex, you are so beautiful!"

She blushed which was for her, to put it mildly, unusual.

"You think so, really?"

"Oh my, yes, my beautiful bride."

Speaking of brides, there was a knock on the door and Margaret and J.D. walked in.

For a second time within minutes, Will's breathing stopped.

Margaret Espinoza, also dressed in a beautiful white dress, had gotten her hair done for the occasion in French braids, and like Alex was wearing just enough make up to make her natural beauty 'pop.' She looked nothing like the Chief of Homicide of the Albuquerque Police Department. J.D. Rawlings was wearing a denim suit that had never come off any rack of any store Will had ever shopped at, wore a coral thunderbird bolo over a white tuxedo shirt, and leather cowboy boots with embroidered turquoise gems. Joining them was J.D.'s brother from El Paso, Bill Rawlings; the Albuquerque Chief of Police, Chuck Dillard; and the Governor of New Mexico, Alfredo Alvarez.

Apparently, Alex knew the Governor was coming and everybody else obviously did too. Will thought he must have missed the memo.

"Thank you all for being here," Judge Kennedy began. "Are you ready to begin?"

Together, J.D. and Margaret, holding hands, nodded 'yes.'

Alex glanced over at Will who was already crying. 'Jesus, just once would he not Shrek himself?' They had once watched the movie *Shrek* together and about half way through she looked over and Will was unabashedly crying. His tears lasted the whole rest of the movie. Time and again, like at the firm after the verdict, he would do that Shrek thing. She loved him all the more for it but really? Could he get a grip? She had asked Grace about it once and she had just laughed. "Alex, every time the two of us watched *E.T.* when I was growing up, he'd cry every time E.T. died. I finally said to him 'Dad, we've seen it seven times. It turns out OK.' And he still cried."

Fortunately, Will was off to the side so the focus could be on Margaret and J.D.

Judge Kennedy started, "With the power vested in me…"

J.D. and Margaret had written their own vows and they repeated them to each other:

"In our lifetimes, we have been witness to great sadness, grief, and sorrow. Without each other, we have endured and been made stronger by what we have seen.

We have also known happiness and hope and love and, together, we will shelter each other from the sorrow and the grief that we have known and cherish the happiness.

We pledge this day that we will love and cherish and worship each other, and when sorrow comes, as it must in life, we pledge we will be together to the end of our days."

So now everybody was Shrekked. Alex asked for the exchange of rings and J.D.'s brother and the governor stepped forward with the rings. They gave them to J.D. and Margaret who placed them on each other's ring fingers.

"I now pronounce you man and wife. You may kiss each other."

And they did. And everybody was still Shrekking.

A champagne toast in chambers that probably violated several county ordinances and hugs all around. Margaret and J.D. were hitched for 'better or for worse.'

At some point during the refill, Will asked the governor how he happened to be in attendance.

"I kept wondering when somebody would ask that question. My original answer was going to be 'I crash weddings all the time, just good campaign politics' but the real reason is Margaret is my god-daughter. Her parents and my wife and I were the best of friends. We don't advertise it especially with her job but we're never far away from each other. Wasn't going to miss this for anything."

Will nodded. Neither would any of them have missed this.

They all adjourned to Antiquity in Old Town that had set aside a room for them. Menu had only one item: Chateaubriand with a Caesar salad with extra anchovies and a baked potato. Red or white wine per the guest. No vegans at this party.

Chapter Forty One
Breaking the Logjam

On cue, Emmett Meyer filed the motion for new trial based on the negligence instruction and a motion for remittitur claiming the jury verdict was far in excess of what was reasonable under the circumstances. In Will's mind, there was no chance for a remittitur based on these facts and the expert testimony. He was more concerned about the negligence instruction although Rosalind McManus' early research indicated they had a good chance based on the testimony of Dr. Dowling and especially Anthony.

A week after the motions were filed but two weeks before Will and Rosalind had to file their answers, Will got a phone call out of the blue.

"Will? Mark Nelson, MISMO. How the hell they hangin'?"

"Mark! Good to hear from you and congrats on the promotion. National Claims Manager. Not much better than that, my friend."

"I'm not sure, Will. A little more money for a lot more headaches. Like calling an old friend who I've known for years who goes over to the 'dark side' in such a spectacular fashion, he hits for $30 million dollars against four dead people. I mean 'What the hell?'"

Will laughed. "You should probably add 'who tortured their son and brother in unspeakable ways all of his life' to 'four dead people.'"

"All kidding aside, Will, you know MISMO, at the end of the day, will never have to pay a dime either on the compensatory or the punitives. Never going to happen."

"You know, if this were Michigan…"

Will heard a heavy sigh. "New Mexico. I get it. I have no idea why we even write insurance in the Land of Enchantment. Certainly not the Land of Enchantment for insurance companies. Still, you've got an uphill climb on the negligence part that potentially triggers the coverage and if we win that, you got nada."

"Two words, Mark. 'New Mexico.'"

"So even though we have a 100% chance of reversal of the verdict, what would it take to settle the case and get it over with?"

"It's $30 million and climbing every day with the interest. And you know that insurance covers the punitive damages and that if you lose the post-trial motions which you will, you'll have to post a bond at a ridiculously high cost. And you know we were willing to settle within policy limits so we get an assignment of the 'bad faith' claim which could trigger MISMO paying the whole verdict. Can't bid against myself, Mark, but I am willing to recommend $30 million dollars to Anthony and his Guardian and drop any claim for interest or costs."

He could almost hear the smile over the phone. "Well, there's a surprise. At this stage I can offer you $3.5 million for the whole shootin' match and an important piece of information that you will take some joy in. Annette Miller is adjusting automobile property damage claims in her home town in Ohio. Great opportunity for her and she doesn't have to travel."

Will's turn to smile. "Well, what a surprise about Ms. Miller. Probably can't tell me but did she just go rogue on this?"

"I'm sorry, Will, I'm not at liberty to say other than you and I have known each other a long time." Which meant she had gone rogue because Nelson was too good at his job to have let this happen if he had known about it.

"$3.5 ain't nearly enough but it's a good faith start. Let me talk it over with the people here and get back with you. Thanks for the call, Mark. Good to talk after all these years."

"Back at you, Will."

Will got hold of Rosalind and Jackie to see if they were free for lunch. They were, although both knew that even though Will would pick up the tab, it would be at a place that served either hot dogs or chicken salad sandwiches or both. Not the Ritz.

It was a beautiful day in mid-June and the decision was made to go to the deli, get sandwiches, and head to Robinson Park for a picnic.

When they got there, they got settled in at a picnic table and Will filled them in on his call with Mark Nelson.

Jackie. "You trust him?"

"I do. Did work for MISMO in Michigan when he was Regional Claims Manager and then again here on cases that came out of his region. Very good guy. Honest. Professional."

"What's he doing working with an insurance company?"

"Despite what you might think, Jackie, not all insurance people wear horns. Mark is one of the exceptions. Last I knew."

Rosalind. "I'm a rookie and things that have all these zeros are a little daunting but it seems like $3.5 million out of the box is pretty serious. If you figure in the land, that nets Anthony somewhere between $2.5 and $3 mil."

"Bullshit. Look what he's been through, Rosalind. A life in hell from the earliest days he can remember. They should pay it all."

"I get it, Jackie, don't shoot the messenger. Point is, it's a reasonable first offer and if we can close it out, we eliminate the appeal and we get him the money now instead of maybe never and maybe in two years."

"So you two, we're at $30 mil and they're at $3.5. Ball's in our court. What, if anything," with a nod towards Jackie, "do we come back with? Take a piece of paper and write down what you think without showing it to anybody and I'll do the same."

The two young women took the paper from Will and thought for a minute. Will had already written his down.

When they were finished writing something down, they looked up and Will said, "OK, what are the numbers?"

Jackie. "$28,500,000."

"Why?"

"We don't want to make a big move until we're certain what their next move is?"

"Will $28.5 million do that or only invite a similar reactionary number? Ponder that for a second. Rosalind?"

"$21,000,000."

"Why?"

“Because, while I’m confident we will win certainly with Judge Peck, there is a chance we could lose on appeal, I think $3.5 was in good faith, and I’d like Anthony to see the money sooner than later. My number sends a signal that we’re serious about settling and we should be. What was yours’s, Will?”

“$25 mil for both of the reasons you give. The average between you two is $24,750,000 and, if the two of you agree, I’m good to go with that with the explanation to Mark Nelson that we think the $3.5 offer is in good faith and therefore we’re willing to move but that we are a little hesitant to go too far too fast.”

Both Rosalind and Jackie were OK with that strategy.

“What about Anthony, Jackie? Should you talk this over with him first?”

“Not at this point. He’s given me full authority and until we see at least the next card from MISMO, we don’t need to talk about it with him. If anything, talking to him about the money just makes him nervous.”

“Think I’ll give it until tomorrow to call Mark back. Don’t want to look too anxious.”

At 11:00 the next morning, noon in Chicago, Will called Mark and told him $24,750,000 for the reasons that both Rosalind and Jackie had talked about.

Will waited for the usual responses from Mark that included, as Will knew they would: “Oh God, there goes the angina again. Now what did I do with the nitroglycerine? Will, you’re killing me. I’ll be out of a job before day’s end. Remember, they are four dead people. Remember? We could win on appeal. No money is enough but enough is enough!”

"Two words, Mark."

"I'll get back with you, Will."

Two days later, Nelson called back.

"Called an emergency board meeting and we met last night. You and I have known each other for a long time and I'm not bull shitting you. We won't pay 'punies.' And whatever you do, don't say 'two words.' Five million."

"I trust you, Mark. Always have. You're one of the really good ones and I respect and admire you for that. Let me get with my folks and see whether they want to roll the dice. Like you said the last time 'no money is enough.' I'll call you back."

Another picnic at Robinson Park with Will, Rosalind, and Jackie. This time they invited Luis Moreno, the other senior litigation member of Johnston & Blackwell, who, with Will and Rosalind and Jackie, made up the plaintiff's personal injury practice group in the firm.

Will filled them all in and once again asked for the numbers confidentially.

Jackie. "$22.5. He's fucked and he knows it. Gives us room to negotiate."

Rosalind. "$14.950 mil. Take it or leave it."

Luis. $14,750 mill. Take it or leave it."

Will thought for a long moment.

"Jackie, talk with Anthony and tell him that we're going to go back one more time and tell the insurance company that we'll take $14,500,000 if it's put on the table. Anything less, game on.

Let me know. Thanks to all of you for everything you've done for this young man."

Late that afternoon, Jackie texted Will: 'Anthony says $14.5 is fine.' He wants closure."

Too late to call Chicago and Will went home. Alex and Will talked about it over a Jameson's and some take out Chinese out on the patio.

"The theme is no amount of money is enough. That's true. MISMO can either continue to make bad law in New Mexico or cut their losses on this one and fight another day. These are terrible facts for the defense and Nelson knows it. You know him well. He must be sick about this case. He's got kids, right?"

Will thought for a minute. "Yes. Two. Close to grown by now."

"Get this one done, my love."

Late morning in late June, the Jiménez v. Jiménez, et al. case settled for $14,500,000 to be paid by MISMO. A week later, Will got a call from the attorney for the life insurance companies offering $250,000 on each of the policies even though only Anthony's brothers were named as beneficiaries and even though the full policies were $500,000 each for Roberto and Esther. After advice and counsel with Jackie and Anthony, Will settled those cases for $300,000 on each of the policies.

Gross numbers at this point were $15,100,000 before fees, liens, and costs. The Representative of the Estates, Peter Flemming, signed a deed granting Anthony the property on Desert Drive to Jackie as Anthony's Guardian and, given its proximity to the irrigation ditch, was immediately listed for sale for $750,000. It sold on the second day it was on the market for $800,000 cash in what turned out to be a bidding war between two farming families farther south down the valley. The listing agent, herself a victim of childhood sexual abuse, took a 2% real estate commission that after closing costs netted $776,000. The buyers said Anthony could stay on the property for the foreseeable future as the primary value was the water, not the house.

Within ten days of the agreements, the checks came from MISMO and the life insurance carriers' checks came in and were put in the firm's trust account.

On July 10, Anthony came to the office and met with Will and Jackie. With a full accounting of fees and costs, the net check they presented to Anthony was for $10,000,000 with another $776,000 that would come with the closing on the Desert Drive real estate. They had put in the settlement agreement with MISMO that some of it could be put into an annuity that would pay out money over time for Anthony's lifetime to make certain no one would try to take advantage of him. They would put $9 million into the annuity that would pay him thousands of dollars over the years and then give him a $1,000,000 'up front' to get what he wanted and they would add the $776,000 to it to provide for alternative housing and continued education and therapy for him.

Will expected some reaction. Joy? Elation? Relief? But there was nothing. At the end, not even a hug or a handshake. Anthony and Jackie left to go to the bank to deposit the money. They would set up a meeting in the next few days with the annuity person to go over the options. It never got done.

Will Bennett would never see Anthony Jiménez alive again.

Chapter Forty Two

Death

A week later, Will got a call from Margaret Espinoza.

"Will, I don't even know how to begin to tell you but Anthony Jiménez killed himself probably sometime yesterday. Jackie stopped by this morning on her way to work and found him in bed. Called 911 and did CPR until the paramedics got there but it was all too late. Probably some kind of overdose that he had been stocking up but we'll need a toxicology screen to be certain. No signs of foul play, a Last Will and Testament, and a note to Jackie.

"Is she there?" Pause.

"Will?"

"Jackie."

"He killed himself, Will." No affect at all. That was scary. "After all he'd been through and after all he'd endured, and with a pot at the end of the rainbow, he killed himself."

"Margaret said he left a will and a note to you. Have you read them?"

"No, police have them and they'll get them to me when they're done."

"Want me there?"

"Josephine's on her way. I'm OK for now. I just don't understand, Will, I. just. don't. understand." A touch of emotion. Good. Very good.

"I'm so sorry, Jackie."

She hung up.

Will called Alex and got Karen because Alex was on the bench.

"I need to talk to her now, Karen. It's important."

She heard it in his voice and said, "Hang on."

A few minutes passed.

"Will?"

"Anthony killed himself. Probably yesterday. Jackie found him this morning."

Silence.

"Fuck me in the heart. How's Jackie?"

"At the house with the police. Josephine's on the way. Left a Last Will and Testament and a letter to Jackie that the police have."

"Need to be there?"

"She says 'no.'"

"Respect it. But, boyfriend, she is gonna need help from all of us down the line."

"Thought you should know as soon as I did. Get back to dispensing what you do best."

"You?"

"Too soon to tell. Something about him that was too good to live in this world." He could feel himself tearing up.

"We'll eat in tonight. Snuggles. It's the way we heal."

"Love you."

"Love you."

"Will?"

"Yep."

"May not feel like it right now but you and your merry band made a big difference in Anthony's life because you gave him justice and gave him standing in the world of humanity. Hold on to that. Promise?"

"Soonly. Maybe. Not there yet." He put his head down and his desk and sobbed until he ran out of tears.

That night was exactly as promised. Snuggles, too much Jameson's, and early to bed. Until about 3:00 when Will woke up, made a pot of coffee, and went out on the patio to wait for the sun to rise.

Chapter Forty Three

Last Will and Testament of Anthony Jiménez

The next morning, Margaret Espinoza stopped by the law firm to drop off the Last Will and Testament as well as the note to Jackie. She gave them both to Will but warned him not to read the letter until Jackie had seen it. He was free to read the Will because Anthony had named Will as the Personal Representative of the Estate. The note to Jackie was private and 'difficult.' He thanked her and asked about a cause.

"The Medical Examiner found what looks like some heroin on the bedside table where Jackie found the body. She's working on the assumption that he may have found some of his brothers' drugs and stashed them to be used at a later time. I think he'd been thinking about this for quite some time, Will. Especially given his note to Jackie. I'll let you know about the drug screen and we should have the results back probably tomorrow."

"Where's the body?"

"Still at the morgue. Once they're done with the autopsy, it will go to Metcalf's Funeral Home." She pointed to the Will. "He wanted to be cremated and leaves it up to you to decide where his ashes should go. He specifically said not at the Desert Drive home. Small wonder there, right?"

"Right."

"Tough stuff, my friend."

"Yep. Thanks, Margaret."

She took a step towards the elevator, stopped, and turned. "She's going to need a lot of help on this, Will. She won't show it, won't express it except maybe to Josephine, but those waters run deep and she loved that boy with a mother's love. She's tough but everybody has a turning point. I know."

"I know you do. We will do whatever it takes for as long as it takes to make her better."

"I know you will. 'Bye."

"'Bye."

Will went back to his office and read the Will. There were going to be some estate tax issues with all the money in the estate but, other than knowing there were going to be some issues, he had no idea what they would be. They would need an accountant to figure that out.

Other than the provisions Margaret had talked about, Anthony had split his entire estate into thirds: one third would go into a suitable foundation that worked with families where sexual abuse victims sought treatment; one third would go into a suitable foundation designed for the diagnosis and treatment of spectrum patients; and one third would go to Jackie LaPointe free and clear, no strings attached.

'Wow. Good for him on all three fronts.' He thought of Dr. Dowling for the sexual abuse bequest and Dr. Davenport for the spectrum bequest. Both could use the money for their work and research and both had gotten to know Anthony which gave the bequests the personal connection. He liked it. And he knew Anthony would too.

He gave some thought to the ashes and where they should be spread. He thought some in a small urn for Jackie and then thought that maybe water would be good. He immediately went to Lake Michigan where some time ago he had spread his best friend's ashes. Anthony had never been anywhere other than Desert Drive and his parents' apartment so it wasn't like Lake Michigan would be any stranger than any other place. Maybe the ocean. He decided he would leave it to Jackie. She would know best. He set the Will down and tried to concentrate on cases that needed some concentrating. Therapeutic.

To his great shock, shortly after the lunch break, Jackie appeared at his office door. Other than a little red in the eyes, she was, for lack of a better word, Jackie. Professional, calm, on the job.

"Margaret dropped off the Will and the note Anthony wrote to you. Asked me not to read it until you had."

She nodded. Will gave her the note in the envelope and she left to go to her office.

Chapter Forty Four

Dear Jackie

Dear Jackie,

By the time you get this, I will be in a better place and finding some peace that I never had until I met you. I will be finding love that I never had until I met you. I know with all of my heart and soul that some time, somehow, some way, our souls shall meet again and I look forward to that time. I know that I will know you no matter what shape or form we take.

I killed them, Jackie, for what they did to me. It was really pretty simple. Once my parents dropped me off at Desert Drive and my brothers locked me in the shed, it didn't take a genius to figure out I could tunnel under the back wall out to the back yard and be free. So that's what I did. I had that done in two weeks after I got there so I had freedom as long as Pablo and José were gone. Then when I knew they were home, I'd tunnel back in the shed and wait for them. There were a couple of close calls but they never suspected. Guess I got the brains of the family. LOL.

When I knew they were gone I'd go in the house just to look around and that's when I found the gun in my parents' bedroom in the closet. I took it back to the shed and hid it knowing someday I would get my revenge.

I watched the whole thing with Maria. I'd get out at night and go peek in the windows and watch her with José and then with Pablo. I could tell she liked Pablo a lot better. I'd never seen sex before. No reason not to tell you now, OK? I would watch her put the perfume on and then climb into bed with Pablo. Then I watched the fight between my brothers and that's when I got the idea.

When those two other guys showed up, it was clear that most of the time, they were all drugged up. And that's when I made my move. Got into the house with the gun, checked in the living room to make sure they were all screwed up, waited for Pablo in the hallway, shot him with the gun using a pillow, drug him into bed, took his clothes off, broke the perfume bottle, scratched 'M' on his chest with part of the bottle, and shoved the other half of the bottle up his ass.

I'm ashamed to say it but that was the best day of my life. Called 911 and you know the rest. I wanted José to burn in hell and I figured everybody would know it was him. Except I had to take the gun and that screwed up the plan big time. Good thing he got his in prison because he deserved every minute of it. That was the third best day of my life when Will told me the news.

The second best day? When I killed my parents. Had their address and walked all the way over with the gun. They were sure surprised to see me. Got them into bed beside each other, shot my father first, and then my mother. Funny. Neither one put up a fuss. Maybe they were just glad it was over. Left the gun there thinking everybody would think it was a murder/suicide.

So that's the whole story and one of the reasons why it has to end like this. As much as I hated all of them for what they did to me, in some strange way, I still loved them. They were all I had until I met you and Will and everybody at the firm. You believed in me.

And the other thing. I'll never be right. I'm funny looking and I can't fix that and people stare at me all the time on the street. I know I'm on the spectrum and, in my lifetime, that won't get fixed. And I know from Dr. Dowling that, given everything that was done to me, I won't ever be normal.

So I'd rather go out like this giving my money to people who care and getting to the other side to see if things will be different. I have to try. I can't go on here.

I know you'll be sad, Jackie, and I'm sad that I'm the one that will cause you to be sad. I'd wish anything not to have you be sad. But you have a beautiful life, a beautiful spouse, and a beautiful future. Live your dreams. Thanks for helping me live mine if only for a little while.

See you on the other side.

I love you,

Anthony

Jackie put the letter down, took a deep breath, and felt a single tear role down her cheek. In her heart of hearts, she knew with near certainty that this was the way it had to end. Years ago, she had been where Anthony was and knew the desolation and loneliness that came with what he'd been through. She had persevered but had nowhere near Anthony's baggage. And she would continue to persevere and knew that Anthony Jiménez, an angel on her shoulder, would make certain she did.

Chapter Forty Five

Good Bye, My Friend

The *Journal* ran an article on Anthony's life and death, under Megan Dixon's byline, with special emphasis on where he wanted the money to go that he had won. Jackie had initially wanted to have a private service but so many people called the office about a service, total strangers, sex abuse survivors, people on the spectrum, that they planned a memorial service at Metcalf's a week after Anthony's death.

Metcalf's had been smart enough to know there would be a crowd but even they underestimated the hundreds of people who came to the service. All of the visitation rooms were in use and with standing room only in most of them. The short service was videoed into the rooms.

The service started with Scripture readings by Jackie LaPointe, Dr. David Dowling, and Dr. Janis Davenport, who had flown in from Boston for the service. The primary eulogy was to be given by Will Bennett. At the end of the readings, that Jackie almost couldn't get through, Will rose to go the lectern.

"Honey," Alex whispered. "Try not to fuck this up." And squeezed his hand.

He looked over the crowd for a moment, took a deep breath, and began.

"In the few short months we had together with Anthony, he taught us all lessons about life that are the most important lessons all of us whose lives he touched have ever learned. They are lessons of courage, of humility, of compassion that we will take to our graves and we are so very grateful for those lessons and for the precious time we had with him."

Will spoke for about twenty minutes about what Anthony had been through and endured and how, finally, he had stood up for humanity and for everyone and had used the justice system to right so many wrongs.

He left out the part about killing his brother and parents thinking it might be a tad much for the congregation. Jackie, Josephine, the Chief of Homicide, J.D., Alex, and Will were the only ones who knew what was in Anthony's note.

At the end, Will ended with what he had said to Alex the night he had learned that Anthony had died.

"There was something about Anthony that was too good to be in this world of ours." He went back to his seat next to Alex. And noted with some satisfaction that he had made her cry. Judging by the sniffles behind him, he had made a few other folks cry as well.

The service ended with Josephine Lucas, Jackie's spouse, vocally trained as a young woman, singing *Goodbye My Friend* by Karla Bonoff.

"Oh we never know where life will take us

We know it's just a ride on the wheel

And we never know when death will shake us

And we wonder how it will feel

So goodbye my friend

I know I'll never see you again

But the time together through all the years

Will take away these tears

It's O.K. now

Goodbye my friend.

But I'm O.K. now

Goodbye my friend

You can go now

Goodbye my friend

Silence for a minute or so and then Will got back up and invited people for coffee outside on the patio at the back of the funeral home. Some of the gathering left but many stayed just to be connected. Will was standing with Alex when a small group of people approached. They looked familiar to him but he couldn't quite place them.

One gentleman came up to him and stuck his hand out and Will shook it.

"I'm Cal Norman. I was the jury foreperson in the trial." He waved behind him. "This is the rest of the jury. When we found out about Anthony's death, we all wanted to be here. Like you said at the service, in his young life, he changed all of ours." Each of them wore teal ribbons in support of victims of sexual abuse.

Will nodded, struggling for words and fighting tears.

Norman put his hand on Will's arm.

"Nothing to say, Will, but know how important this young man was to us and to all of these people. Keep doing what you're doing." Each of the other six jurors and the alternates came up to Will and hugged him.

"Given what we've been through, we've stayed in touch and we're going out to lunch together today. Do it about once a month now." The others nodded. "We'll raise a glass."

Will nodded again, still without finding words, and the jury dispersed.

Several other people came up to him and said much the same thing. A sexual abuse survivor said she had followed the trial and was so proud of Anthony for standing up for himself. She said it gave her courage to believe that there was a future for her even after what she'd been through.

The crowd thinned and Margaret Espinoza and J.D. Rawlings came up to Will and Alex with a very attractive young woman with them.

"Judge Kennedy and Will, we'd like you to meet Maria Thompson." Both of them recognized the name as the runaway who had gone to the police to testify against her former boyfriend José Jiménez in the murder trial.

"Very nice to meet you, Maria. You're a very brave young woman," said Alex. Will nodded.

"I wanted to be here to pay my respects. I never met Anthony while I was at the house but followed the story. I'm so sorry."

"Thanks for saying something." Will.

"Before we leave, Maria, maybe these two would like to know what you're doing these days."

Maria looked at both of them. "With Margaret's help, I got into a half-way house for homeless people. Been there a few months. I'm full time at the community college working towards a degree in substance abuse counseling. Plus I'm working at the local Narcotics Anonymous chapter. Everything that happened I think happened in part for me to finally see myself. I'm grateful for that."

Alex hugged her and Will shook her hand.

"Wishing you the very best, Maria."

"Thank you both."

She left with J.D. and Margaret and Will looked at his spouse. "Every once in a while, things can turn out OK. Got to keep holding on to that."

"Yep."

Will saw Jackie and Josephine across the funeral home at the altar and went up to them.

"Want to come over tonight for a cook out?"

"I think Jackie and I are going to head to the mountains for a few days, Will. Got to sort some things out and getting away would be a good thing. Heading out now."

Will looked at Jackie who nodded at him.

"I'll be all right, Will. What you said was perfect. As much as I miss him, I know my life is fuller because of him." She smiled. "And boy, did he take care of business or what? I call that major revenge."

He smiled, too. "You saved him, Jackie. Not forever because he couldn't be saved given what he'd been through but you gave him joy and love and compassion that he had never experienced before. Hold on to that, OK?"

She hugged him good bye. "OK, Chief. See you in a couple of days."

Will reported to Alex that they were being stood up for dinner. She reached for her cell phone and punched in a number.

"Margaret, Alex. You and J.D. want to come over for a barbecue tonight?"

She listened for a second. "Great. See you about 6:00. No need to bring anything but your own sweet selves." She hung up and looked at Will.

"Sorry. Should have asked but I don't think being alone tonight would be good for either of us."

"Agree 100%. Great idea." He checked his watch. "Trader Joe's?"

"Perfect. Let's blow this pop stand."

Chapter Forty Six

Requiem

Will had loved to grill all his life but, sadly, even he had to admit that his efforts, at best, were about a C+. It wasn't for lack of trying, or grilling cookbooks, or thermometers, or the right grill but, more often than not, his product either turned out to be sushi which is not something that's good when you're cooking chicken or hard enough to be an insole in a shoe for somebody with flat feet. He was to barbecuing what Alex was to breakfast.

So when they got to Trader Joe's, they found an already cooked package of ribs that required only heating up. Alex promised him that he could use the grill to warm them up as long as it was done under close supervision by a responsible adult. They added corn on the cob, coleslaw, and some garlic bread. Several bottles of wine found their way into the basket, some strawberries that they would pour some cognac over for dessert, and they were out the door.

On the way home, Alex very quietly said, "You hit a home run today, slugger."

"Thanks, Alex. He was amazing. And all the more so given what he did to his brother and parents. You feel like he should be blamed but what I'm really doing is standing on the sidelines cheering my head off for justice."

"Margaret and J.D.'s take will be interesting."

They arrived right on the dot and instructions notwithstanding brought some snacks and a couple of bottles of wine.

And overnight bags.

"Probably we should have announced that we might be staying the night and maybe we won't but we'd rather not have either J.D. or me being arrested for a DWI."

Alex mentally checked off that the guest room had clean sheets.

"Excellent! A slumber party! Breakfast at the Western View. What can we get you for starters?"

A vodka martini, two Jameson's, and a glass of white wine later, they were out on the patio.

Alex raised her glass. "To Anthony and all that he taught us."

The others raised their glasses and clinked and drank.

"So now what, ABQ Chief of Homicide?"

Margaret. "Well, with no help from anybody but Anthony, we solved three murders with the suicide note. Case closed."

Will asked, "Any chance of some heir suing for money?"

"Lawyers will sue for anything but I can't imagine. Sexually abused for years by parents and brothers and the two sisters in Mexico want money? Rots of Ruck. Shoot, Will, even you could win that case." J.D. with a smile. And an empty glass.

"Appreciate your confidence, J.D. But I agree. Does it need to be public that he confessed to the murders?"

Margaret now. "J.D. and I have talked a lot about that and, unfortunately, we think the answer is 'yes.' To do anything else would invite cover up allegations if it ever came out. Always the cover up, right? So our collective wisdom, we announce we have closed the cases with Anthony's note. Trouble is we may get copy cats from even some of the people who were at the memorial service today who will go on vendettas against their abusers. Not that they don't deserve it…if it's true. But that's not good either. Any way you look at it, there are plenty of moving parts."

Will went in the house and returned with refills.

The judge weighed in. "My vote and I don't have a vote and this is confidential and I hope nobody is wired but my opinion is that it all comes out. Yes, it may create copycat killers but it might also help victims come forward with courage and not violence."

Will nodded to make it unanimous.

The rest of the evening devolved into getting served too much, talking about Anthony, talking about Jackie, talking about life. At one point Will looked at the three and thought to himself 'what an odd coupling. Liberal as hell Will and Alex, Chief of Homicide for the ABQ Police Department, and a prosecutor who is a lifer.' And they truly liked each other.

Alex saw the look in Will's eyes. "Don't go Shrek on me, Will."

"I'll get the ribs ready." Like he had to do anything more than warm them up.

'Geez, please don't put the barbecue apron and hat on,' Alex thought to herself.

But he didn't and, almost unbelievably, he warmed them just enough to be hot without cooking them to leather. Dinner was great and made even better by the consumption of two or three bottles of wine and some after dinner Jameson's neat.

"Well, Martha, let's you and me get to bed. I'm sure these people need to get home."

"Will, it's 9:00 and they're spending the night."

"Oh, right. Well, Martha, let's get to bed. I'm sure these people need to get up early and get to work."

"It's Saturday night and we're going to have breakfast at the Western View after we sleep in."

"Well, Martha, I'm pretty much up to my gills in alcohol and will make it upstairs OK if nobody steps on my hand."

"Don't forget to take the Tylenol tonight, Will."

He forgot. And was joined soon after by his bride, with J.D. and Margaret in the guest room.

"What a wonderful night, Alex, just what we needed." Will slurred and rolled over.

That meant she'd need the earplugs for sure.

"What a great night, Margaret, just what we needed." J.D. slurred and rolled over.

Margaret hoped like hell she'd packed the earplugs.

11:00 Sunday morning at the Western View was a bit subdued for the foursome. Not in any great pain but moving very slowly. Huevos rancheros Christmas for Alex and J.D. and Breakfast Burritos with extra onions, sausage, and green chili for Will and Margaret.

"Did we solve the world's problems last night?"

"No, Will, but we did some healing for some stuff we've been through over the last several months and that deserved a blowout. Moderation only goes so far."

Alex asked a question that had been bothering her since it had happened.

"Margaret. Regrets over the death of the Tenderloin Killer, Desmond Allen?"

"Not for a heartbeat. He deserved to die for what he did and he did the right thing by killing himself. That case is closed." No need to go into details. Alex knew better than to go any further.

One more time. "To Anthony." Coffee mugs raised and touched.

Chapter Forty Seven

Ashes to Ashes

In late June, sort of out of the blue, Jackie stuck her head in Will's office and asked about a picnic at Robinson Park and said she'd even buy. A first.

Since the verdict, as had been the practice after the Ruiz verdict, the firm had been inundated with potential new cases and Jackie and Rosalind had been put in charge of screening them and conducting preliminary interviews. Not surprisingly, a number of the cases had to do with sexual abuse… family members, members of the clergy, almost always someone known to the victim, etc. The problems in most of them were twofold: first, they had happened so long ago that the time had expired by which a lawsuit could be filed and, second, collectability from the abusers was nigh on to impossible. They had gotten lucky in Anthony's case because of the mistakes made by the MISMO adjuster and because it was New Mexico law that controlled. On the other hand, there were two or three that were both within the time frame and the abusers had some assets that could be collected on.

They stopped at the deli, loaded up on sandwiches and dill pickles, and some sodas and headed for the park. Jackie was uncharacteristically quiet on the trip over and they found a table and set up.

"Couple of things I need to tell you, Will."

He nodded.

"First," and she pulled out a baggie filled with a white substance that Will hoped to hell wasn't cocaine. "These are some of Anthony's ashes and I'd like you to scatter them on the waters of Lake Michigan the next time you're there."

He took the baggie and nodded again.

"The rest of the ashes we're putting in places that strike Josephine and me he would have liked. Took some to the mountains and found a beautiful place in a meadow with a great view; we have kept some for us; we put some on the Rio Grande and hope that it would help get him back to his homeland somehow; and here's a small wooden box that we thought you might want to keep for yourself." She handed over a beautiful wooden carved box maybe four inches by six inches. "Don't know how you feel about things like this but you were so important to him, we thought it would be a nice thing."

Will still hadn't said a word, the sandwich left untouched on the table.

"I know you talked about Lake Michigan and I really like the idea of his soul being able to float but we wanted to do some other things as well."

Will cleared his throat. "I'll take care of Lake Michigan and I'll treasure these ashes." Pointing to the box. "He was every bit as important to me as I was to him."

"A second thing I want to tell you is about the money. As you know, we got Dr. Dowling and Dr. Davenport set up with non-profit foundations and their share of the money is already deposited with them. I talked to both of them yesterday and they have set up small Boards that will oversee disbursements. I'm on both Boards."

He was back to nodding.

"As for my share, Josephine and I have set up the Lucas LaPointe Foundation also as a non-profit and have funded it initially with $2.3 million. We're not sure what we're going to use it for yet but will let it grow and decide as time goes on."

Jackie stopped and took a deep breath.

"The rest we're going to invest for us…and our child. Josephine's pregnant. She's a girl and we're naming her Antonia. We'll call her Noni."

He looked at her for a long time. She'd come a hell of a long way since that time she had worked as a tattooed and pierced techie for the Alexandria Police Department.

"Anything else? Lettuce on my sandwich is beginning to wilt."

"No, Will."

Halfway through lunch, he looked up at her.

"Did you ever consider 'Wilamena?'"

"Not even for a heartbeat. Sorry. But we are hoping you and Alex will be her godparents if that's any consolation."

He nodded again. "Be proud and honored." He stopped for a second to take a deep breath so as not to become a blubbering mass of protoplasm. "You two will be incredible parents."

Now it was Jackie's turn to nod.

Epilogue

J.D. and Margaret had finally gotten to go on the honeymoon they had put off for months. On the recommendation of friends, they booked a suite at the La Pensione Hotel in the Little Italy area of San Diego. Great neighborhood, lots of good restaurants, lots of loving. A respite they both needed.

The last night before getting back to Albuquerque, they were at their favorite restaurant they'd found, Buon Apppetito. They finished the first margarita.

"Margaret?"

She looked up.

"How could they have been watching the same show on TV when the power was off?"

She looked at the love of her life for a long second. And then turned to the waiter. "Two more, please."

"Yes, ma'am."

She raised her hand. "Make them doubles, would you?"

This is Bill's fifth novel and, as much as he loves writing them, he isn't giving up his day job as a mediator and arbitrator in West Michigan. He and Rebecca live in Grand Rapids with various and sundry rescue animals except for the winter when Rebecca announces, "you people are crazy to live here" and concentrates on her law practice in Albuquerque.